Hart Mountain Hotshots Series
BOOK 7

Rest less
GAY SHIFTER EROTIC FICTION
SPIRITS

WARNING

This book contains sexually explicit scenes and adult language. It may be considered offensive to some readers. This book is for sale to adults ONLY.

Please store your files wisely where they cannot be accessed by underage readers.

* * * * * * * * * * * * * * * * * *

WANT FREE COPIES OF MY BOOKS?
Just visit my blog and download free copies of my books:
http://angus-macgregor.awesomeauthors.org/angus-macgregor/

About the Publisher

4Fun Publishing, a member of **BLVNP Incorporated**, 340 S. Lemon #6200, Walnut CA 91789, info@blvnp.com / legal@blvnp.com
NOTE: Due to the highly emotional reaction of some people to works of erotic fiction, any email sent to the above address that contains foul language or religious references is automatically deleted by our anti-spam software and will not be seen. All other communications are welcome.

DISCLAIMER

Hart Mountain Hotshots Series, Book 7

Restless Spirits

Gay Shifter Erotic Fiction

By: Angus MacGregor

ISBN: 978-1-68030-574-6

Chapter 1

Eli pulled his fire pack onto his sturdy back and grabbed his duffle bag off the carousel and looked around the deserted baggage claim area. It was 2:30 in the morning and he was groggy and stiff, but his belly fluttered with excitement. He just got the call from his dispatch center to head to the Black Crater fire in Oregon. He had only been on two smaller fires in Wisconsin besides his training burns. He had missed out getting on a crew but decided to sign up as an AD firefighter. His center manager told him that with the fire season heating up so fast, he was bound to get picked up by a crew that needed a replacement.

Sure enough, the call came through yesterday afternoon. A hotshot crew based in the Willamette valley was currently working a fire in Central Oregon near Bend. One of the crew had a family medical emergency and had to leave quickly. Just the kind of break that Eli was hoping for. He had headed to Marquette from the bustling metropolis of Christmas, Michigan - population 400. The town hardly existed other than from Thanksgiving to New Year's. Then the population exploded right along with the prices in the souvenir shops and tourist traps. It was Algonquin land, Ojibwa to be more exact. But the tribes had lost most of it to the Feds even though they were currently working on getting some of it back, one pull of the slot machine handle at a time. It was Eli's first time out of the Upper Peninsula region of Michigan as well as his first plane ride. The last year of his life had been hell on earth, but the universe was smiling on him again.

He was a strong, solidly built Native American guy. He was almost twenty-two years old, but only looked about eighteen. His upper arms were bulging, stretching the cotton of his red t-shirt. His long black hair hung to his shoulders. His eyes were the color of cinnamon framed by thick, black eyebrows and long lashes. His face was smooth with only a dusting of a mustache peeking out from his lip. His legs were muscled and thick, and his ass looked like a damn black girl booty, at least that was what his friends said. Most other Indian guys he knew had a scrawny flat ass, but his was round and meaty.

Eli got to the airport almost three hours before his flight. Luckily, he could check his bags and not have to pay the expensive fees. He wandered around the small airport in Marquette, looking for some food. There was only a convenience store and the choices were slim and mostly disgusting. But, he bought a sandwich and a Coke and made the best of it. He went to the bathroom to wash some mustard off his hands. The place was deserted except for a tired-looking business man trying to get a stain off his tie. He glanced up at Eli and smiled.

"This place sucks balls at night," the man said.

"It's pretty quiet, that's for sure."

"I come through here about once every two months. It's always this way. I've wondered if I could just walk around without my pants on and see if anyone would even notice."

Eli laughed. "That's funny."

"So where are you headed? You look like a firefighter or something."

"Yeah, I am. Heading to Oregon," Eli said walking over to the urinal. His large Coke was calling.

"I heard they had some big fires. Well, good for you." The man casually adjusted his crotch through his slacks and walked over to stand beside Eli. He didn't skip a john even though there were six in a row. Eli could tell the man was staring at his junk and it made him smile. He stepped back a bit and opened up his Nomex pants wide and pulled out his cock and balls, and let them flop. He held his hands on his hips, watching his piss splash into the urinal along with the businessman's fixed gaze. Eli looked over and saw the man's short, stubby penis hard and standing out straight from his furry belly. The man slid his thick foreskin back and forth over the red tip, slowly licking his lips as he watched Eli urinate. Unnoticed to the businessman, Eli's face trembled and shifted into a new shape. His hair lightened in color and hairs slowly sprouted on his chest under his t-shirt.

"I had to piss like a race horse," Eli said, looking over at the man.

"Yeah. That's pretty impressive," the man said. He looked around and then back down at Eli's cock. "Could I...?" The man asked, reaching over toward Eli. He gripped Eli's penis with a warm hand and slowly jacked it back and forth.

"Fuck, you are huge buddy," the man said as Eli's penis grew to its full length. "Holy shit, that's a beautiful cock, kid." The man looked up from stroking Eli's dick and a quizzical expression crossed his face. "It's funny. I could have sworn you had dark hair." The man pushed up Eli's t-shirt and rubbed the now furry, flat belly. "Nice fur, buddy."

Eli pulled his shirt up farther, enjoying the curly blond hairs that now grew from his crotch up his belly, to his chest. He grinned and looked at the businessman who still slowly stroked his penis.

"You look like that guy. You know, the one from Parks and Rec and Jurassic World."

"You mean Chris Pratt?"

"Yeah. You look just like him."

"Well. He's pretty good-looking, so thanks. Um, you're just gonna keep jacking me off or…" Eli said with a grin.

"Any chance I could suck you off?"

Eli looked around and shrugged. "Go into the stall, man."

The businessman picked up his rolling bag and moved into the large stall. He pushed his pants down to his ankles and sat on the toilet, legs spread wide, his cock hard and pointed to the ceiling. Eli followed him in, leaving his dick hanging out, bouncing. He locked the door and grabbed the man's head and pressed it into his crotch. He grinned as his leaking cock left a trail of honey on the man's face as he rubbed his meat on his cheeks, nose, and lips. The man opened his mouth and Eli slid his now massive cock into his eager throat. He gagged and his eyes watered, but he adjusted and soon began to do a respectable job of sucking, while Eli gripped his head and thrust in and out, smiling at the man's gurgles and muffled grunts. He felt his balls get ready to release and he forced his dick's full length into the wet mouth and unloaded his nut deep within. A deep, rumbling growl, almost cougar-like, echoed off the tile walls. Eli pulled his dick back and shook off the last drops of semen and tucked it back in his shorts. He held his hand to the side of the man's head, and smiled his best Chris Pratt look-alike smile.

"Thanks, brother. Have a good night."

Eli unlocked the door and looked around before heading out of the bathroom, smiling as he listened to the smacks of the businessman masturbating in the stall. *This night is already better than I expected,* he thought. As he walked the gate waiting area, his face shimmered again and it slid into his regular dark, smooth features. He watched the businessman leave the bathroom a few minutes later and look his way before heading down the corridor, looking for the Jurassic movie star.

The flight was easy and quiet in the 50-passenger small plane. Eli sat on one of the back rows and actually got both seats to himself. He scooted around and slept for the biggest part of the flight, his hand tucked inside the waistband of his pants like he always did. He was groggy and bleary-eyed when he got to the Redmond airport. He grabbed his gear and looked around and saw a big, strapping blond guy in a form-fitting t-shirt and well-worn Nomex pants standing near the exit with a sign that read ELI BUNGO, hastily scrawled on a torn piece of cardboard. Actually, the sign had read: ELI BUNGHOLE, with the H-L-E carelessly crossed out. Eli smirked. *He'd never heard that joke before,* he thought. *Funny guys here like back home.*

"Hey, I'm Eli," he said, stretching out his hand to the husky, blond guy holding the sign.

The man's face lit up when he saw Eli. "Hey there, buddy. Looks like you found me. I'm Jesse. Jesse Patterson. I'm an Engine Boss at Hart Mountain Hotshots. Welcome to the suck."

"Hey. I'm grateful for the opportunity," Eli said as Jesse easily grabbed up his duffle bag and slung it on his shoulder.

"Let's see if you still feel that way in two weeks," Jesse chuckled. "Glad we found a newbie willing to ride with us. Not everyone will."

Eli wondered what a cryptic message like this was supposed to mean, but he just shrugged and smiled. "I needed the work, bro, so I am happy to be part of the Hart Mountain crew." Eli walked faster to keep up with Jesse's big strides. *Shit,* he thought, *I wouldn't mind bunking with Thor here.*

They climbed into a crew cab pickup, tossing Eli's gear into the truck bed. Jesse punched the accelerator and took off toward the town of Redmond. The air was smoky and still in the cool, night air.

"Smells like the fire isn't too far away from here," Eli said.

"Believe it or not, it's more than fifty miles away. But it's a big motherfucker, over 50,000 acres right now and running. Did you get any sleep on the plane?"

"A little, you know how it goes," Eli said, acting as if he knew everything about airline travel. He figured his act would get sniffed out easily, so he kept it short and sweet.

"Well, I've been up for more than 16 hours already. Day shift starts in less than three hours so there is no way we are going to make it back and get rested for our shift. Jake, that's our crew boss, told us to just stay here in Redmond and get some sleep. He was going to transition all the crew to the night shift for a few days. You hungry? You want to hit Denny's or something before we hit the hay?"

"Sure, yeah, that sounds good."

Ten minutes later, the guys were shoveling down hot Grand Slams, complete with eggs, pancakes, hash browns, and grits. Jesse ate like a starving castaway, working his way through the food in no time at all. Eli liked the guy. He was a pretty normal guy, not a macho shithead and not some city slicker either.

"So, you're an Indian?" Jesse asked with no discretion at all. *So much for me thinking this guy was cool*, Eli thought.

"Yeah. Ojibwa. Part of the Algonquin nation."

"That's cool. The guy you're replacing is an Indian too. I don't know what tribe he's from. His name was Big Farmer. You know him?"

Eli laughed. "Can't say that I do." Eli watched as Jesse grabbed the crotch of his pants and pulled them down, lifting his ass off the seat.

"God, I am tired of wearing these fucking pants. Squeezing my sack like a sack of oranges. Can't wait to get out of them and these goddamn boots."

Eli agreed with a quick, "Yeah, I hear you." *I wouldn't mind seeing you out of those pants myself,* he thought. As the truck moved closer to the lights of the town, Eli thought, *Better be cool, jackass. This big ox could probably do some damage to you if he thought you wanted to see his dick.*

Jesse pulled up to the Comfort Suites and jumped out of the truck. "I'll go get our room. Be right back. You can just chill." Eli nodded. He waited until Jesse was inside and slid his hand into his pants and adjusted his package. His cock was more than half-hard and was leaking pre-cum into his shorts. He pulled his hand back out and licked his finger. *Get hold of yourself, you fool. These white boys are gonna kick your red ass.*

Jesse got back in the truck with a sour expression on his face. "Ass clowns," he muttered, starting up the Ford.

"What's up?"

"Ah, they fucked up the reservation." Jesse's face reddened and he giggled. "Sorry, man." Eli roared.

"You are one funny guy, bro."

"There's still a room for us, but it's a fuckin' queen bed. We have to double up all the time but I was hoping for more room so we could stretch out. Oh well, guess we'll just have to cuddle instead. Hope you like firefighter balls rubbing against your ass all night, Eli."

"I'm so tired you could put your sack on my face and I wouldn't even know it."

"Oh you'd know it, amigo. I've got some big brass balls," Jesse said gripping his crotch. Eli laughed.

The firefighters found their room and stood, looking at the tiny bed.

"Fuck me, I think this is a double bed. Shit. Which side you want?" Jesse asked annoyed.

"Don't matter. This one's fine," he said sitting his duffle bag on the right side of the bed. Jesse dropped to the mattress and began to unlace his boots, pulling them off with a clunk. The room filled with the funk of damn, sweaty feet and armpits. "Uh, you can grab the shower first if you want," Eli offered.

"You had enough of my stank already, Cochise? Is it okay to call you that? I'm not trying to be racist," Jesse said, pulling his shirt off and tossing it to the floor. His chest was furry and blond, and Eli was reminded of his bathroom fling in Marquette.

"Cochise was an Apache. Kind of like confusing you with Tony Soprano."

"Look who just grew a pair. Dude, I was just busting your balls. By the way, don't let anyone pull that racist shit with you. The crew doesn't stand for that really," Jesse reached over and pulled Eli into a big hug, gripping his head with his arms and pulling his nose into his pits. Eli pushed away, coughing.

"Fuck, white boys can really stink, brother," he said with a laugh.

"You ain't smelled nothing yet. I'm like roses compared to some of our crew." Jesse unfastened his pants and pulled them and his socks off. Eli stared at the full basket in his white briefs. He watched Jesse bend down and fish out a fresh pair of underwear from a backpack. He slid the briefs off his round ass and headed to the bathroom. "I'll leave the door open in case you need to piss or take a dump," he said as he disappeared into the shower.

Eli unlaced his boots and laid them against the wall. He draped his socks over the top so they would dry off a bit. He took off his shirt and folded it up along with his pants. He thought about it for a minute, then slid his boxer briefs off and stood in front of the mirror to brush his teeth, naked. *Might as well show this white boy I can hang with the best of them,* he thought. The leather strap and amulet hung around his neck close to his smooth chest in between his quarter-sized dark, brown nipples. He touched it and closed his eyes.

"Nimishomis." I miss you. Guide my path, Papa. Help me remember your words and the lessons you taught. Thank you and the Great Spirit for this chance. Keep me strong. Keep me safe. Bless my new brothers, especially Jesse.

"Amen, Cochise," a deep voice behind him said, laying a warm hand on his shoulder. Eli's eyes opened and Jesse stood behind him wearing a towel. His short cropped blond hair full of water, his blue eyes sparkling. "Shower's all yours, bro."

Eli ducked his head, feeling embarrassed and way too naked. He walked into the bathroom and closed the door. The air was moist and close. He turned on the shower and stepped inside, enjoying the water sliding over his skin. He picked up a bottle of Axe shower gel and lathered up his chest and pits, washing his belly and balls before sliding a finger up into his ass and rinsing the suds away. He stuck his head under the water and used the hotel shampoo and lathered up his long, dark hair. He pulled back the shower curtain and almost screamed. Jesse was there brushing his teeth. He hadn't even heard him come in. *This guy might have some Indian blood in him if he can move that quietly,* he thought. Eli noticed Jesse checking out his dick as he toweled off. A tremble moved in his belly that he tried to calm down. He felt the flush of blood fever move through him, but it was more than a week before the full moon. He walked into the bedroom and slid on some new boxer briefs and brought back his toothbrush. Jesse was washing off his mouth, spitting the toothpaste into the sink. He pulled back so Eli could wet his toothbrush. Jesse stood almost a head taller than Eli. He put his hands on Eli's shoulders and gave them a light squeeze.

"Didn't mean to interrupt your prayer time, Cochise."

Eli looked at the big blond boy and decided right then and there the big lug didn't mean anything mean or hateful with his nickname. "No problem, Thor. You can pray with me anytime."

Jesse grinned and reached around to hug Eli from behind. "Thor. I like that, Cochise. We're gonna be buds for sure." With that, Jesse actually smacked Eli on the side of the face with his lips before smacking his round ass. "Come on, Geronimo. Let's get in bed. I am so dead."

"Geronimo was Apache, too, Dickhead," Eli said. Jesse laughed heartily from the bedroom.

"Hurry up, sweetheart. It's cold in here without you. I turned the A/C down too far."

Eli rolled his eyes but grinned. He took a quick piss before heading out to the bedroom. Jesse completely filled up the entire bed with his big bulk. Eli tried to slide into his side of the bed without crashing into the other firefighter, but the boy grabbed him and pulled him close.

"No need to be shy, honey. Fuck, you are solid as a tank," Jesse said, pulling Eli close. Jesse slid his arm under Eli's shoulders and Eli laughed and laid his head on Jesse's arm. "You are a pretty affectionate guy, Jesse. Or are you just busting my balls?"

"Little of both, buddy. Speaking of balls, you got some big ones, Chief Joseph." Jesse's hand slid down and casually patted Eli's crotch, gripping his sack and giving his testicles a light squeeze. Eli followed suit and wrapped his hand around Jesse's ample package and squeezed.

"I never knew Euro twink boys had big dicks, either," he said.

"Oh you're gonna pay for that one," Jesse said rolling on top of Eli, wrestling him flat to the mattress, pinning him down. Jesse pushed hard on Eli's arms, holding them on top of the pillow, smashing his big frame onto the smaller young man. Eli could feel Jesse's erection pressing against his own. The blond firefighter's face was hovering right above his. He could feel the warm toothpaste breath on his face. Eli felt the bloodlust boil in his belly, lighting up his eyes. A low cougar-like growl purred from his throat. Jesse froze.

"How the hell did you do that?" Jesse asked, almost in a whisper.

"What?" Eli said, playing dumb.

"That sound. That growl in your throat. That was wicked, man."

"Not sure. Guess it's just being so tired or something. Um, you wanna get off me? You weigh a ton, bro."

Jesse laughed and rolled off Eli and pulled him back close, wrapping his arm around him. He laid a hand on Eli's smooth belly, dangerously close to his junk. His cock was growing fat and stiff. *What's up with this guy?* Eli thought. Part of him felt the urge to pull away and roll to his side of the bed, but the bigger part of him settled into the embrace, soaking in the warm, sensual vibes put off by this big goob.

"So how much you know about Hart Mountain Hotshots, brother?"

Eli shifted his leg so it pressed directly against Jesse's. "Not much. Honestly, I'd never heard of it until yesterday when I got the dispatch. I figured it was just a good crew, you know."

"You got that right, man. We're the best. But we are kind of, um, different, mostly in regard to after-hours stuff and what we do for fun, you know, all that."

Eli turned in the bed. His face was looking right at Jesse now. *Goddamn, Thor. You are making me crazy here. If your hand gets any closer to my dick...* "Okay, well I guess I'm curious about what that means. You guys deal drugs or do devil worship or something?"

Jesse laughed. "Nah, nothing that crazy. We're just sort of different than most other crews."

Eli smiled. "Different how? I mean, other than wanting to fuck me and all that."

"That obvious, huh?"

"Dude, your hand is practically holding my dick, and you have been perving on me since we met. Are you trying to say you guys are a gay crew or something?"

Jesse grinned. "Let's just say we're close."

"So, you all fuck each other?"

"Pretty much, yeah. How do you feel about that, buddy?"

"What happens if I'm not into it?"

"Nothing. I mean, you probably are going to have a hard time not seeing other guys from the crew hooking up. And I won't promise they wouldn't hit on you from time to time. But, no one is a d-bag and gonna rape your boyhole or something."

I'd love to see them try, Eli thought. "So, all twenty guys are queer?"

"Not really. I mean, some of the guys for sure are just out and out gay. A couple are even married. But, we also have some bi guys and even some guys married to women who like to play during fire season. Right now, we don't really have any guys who are hands down not interested. Guess we just sort of attract guys who want some dick now and then…or all the time, more often than not," Jesse said with a chuckle. His hand moved down Eli's belly and gripped his semi-hard cock. "Seems like you might be okay with it. You ever tried dick before?"

Eli reached over and slid his hand inside Jesse's briefs and felt the thick penis resting on his furry sack. "Couple of times. Might be okay," was his short answer as his face moved closer to Jesse's. Jesse's hand moved into Eli's shorts and gripped his cock. His thumb moved across his piss slit and he slid the wetness around Eli's dickhead.

"Holy shit, rookie. That's an awesome dick."

Eli pushed Jesse's shorts down under his balls and off his round ass. Jesse followed suit and the firefighters ground their dicks against one another as they wrapped their arms lightly around each other's thick shoulders, their faces rubbing on one another. Jesse's lips ran down Eli's cheek and found his mouth. His hot tongue lightly parted Eli's lips and slipped inside. Jesse's fingers found Eli's smooth ass crack and slid down the smooth skin until they found his warm boyhole. Jesse teased and tickled Eli's hole as they kissed long and hard.

"I am way too fucking tired for this," Jesse said, "But goddamn, rookie. We won't have a bed again for two weeks."

"Too much talking. More fucking," Eli said, pushing Jesse back and pushing his big legs far apart, taking his hard cock into his mouth all the way down to the thick, blond pubes.

"Shhhhiit!" Jesse said, gripping Eli's head and thrusting deep into his mouth. "Fuck, how are you taking all of that so easily, rook? I almost always gag Brandon."

As Eli sucked, a river of saliva poured from this mouth that looked more like a crazed, rabid animal now. His face was elongated somehow as he slid the whole eight inches of Jesse's penis easily into his ravenous mouth. His tongue lapped at the blond firefighter's full sack as well. Jesse grabbed his ankles and pulled his legs wide apart. Eli's fingers, slick with saliva, slid into Jesse's fuzzy hole in one slow motion.

"Holy God," Jesse groaned. "Fuck me, rookie. How big are your fucking fingers?"

Eli's fingers swelled and grew longer as he pushed two of them deeper and deeper into Jesse's ass as he sucked. A low rumble, almost like a lion, purred from Eli's full mouth, reverberating against Jesse's hard cock.

"Christ. How are you doing that? Oh my God, kid."

Eli pulled out of Jesse's ass and climbed up and pushed his fat cock into Jesse's mouth. Eli's penis was shockingly erect now, almost twelve inches of Ojibwa meat, leaking and thick. Jesse's eyes practically popped out of his head as Eli's dick slid into his mouth. Eli grabbed Jesse's head and began to skull fuck him fast and hard. The blond firefighter gagged and pushed against the impossible cock, but Eli held fast and continued the pumping. Jesse's eyes watered but he grabbed Eli's smooth brown ass and pulled him tighter to his face, retching and gagging.

Eli pulled out of Jesse's mouth and flipped the big guy over like a toy, spreading his ass apart and driving his tongue deep into the dusty brown muscle. Jesse groaned and pushed his ass up hard against Eli's face. Eli milked Jesse's cock and balls as he ate his hole until it was sopping wet. He clambered between his legs and rested the tip of his swollen cock against the wet pucker.

"This is gonna hurt, brother," Eli said with a low growl. "Bite that pillow, buddy." He leaned into Jesse's ass and parted the tight ring and slid in four inches hearing him cry out into the pillow. He readjusted and slid the rest of his length inside his new crewmate. When he was balls deep into the big boy's manhole, he rested his body on top of the firefighter feeling his sphincter grip and contract around his cock. It was intoxicating. God, he loved this feeling, penetrating a brother like this and breeding him. Eli's face was almost totally animal now, covered with fur. His belly had sprouted hair and his fingernails were claws. He rutted hard into Jesse, mating with him. He drove his full length into his hole again and again while Jesse cried out in pain and delight. Eli felt his seed boil inside his balls. He gripped Jesse's shoulders and thrust one last time, and flooded his ass with semen. It came and came, bubbling out the edges of the blond boy's hole in large, white rivers of cream. It took all of Eli's strength not to roar, not to rip, not to kill. He collapsed on top of Jesse, his face and body resuming their normal shape and size. Jesse's hole was open and oozing with sperm, leaking and coating his furry sack. Jesse pushed Eli off him and spun around with a shocked, almost angry look on his face. But he took one look at Eli and grabbed his head, and force-fed him his thick cock, pumping hard and fast into the smaller boy's mouth until he grunted in release, forcing his cum into Eli's mouth. The sperm leaked from the corners of his mouth and dripped onto his smooth chest, as Jesse pumped more and more seed into him. He gripped his penis and caught the stray drops on the corners of Eli's mouth, and forced them back into the boy's mouth until he had devoured every drop. Jesse fell back on the bed, his chest heaving. Eli climbed up and fell onto Jesse's belly, listening to the boy's breathing and heartbeat slow down as his hands caressed his long black hair.

An hour later, Eli woke. Jesse was quietly snoring, holding on to him like a little boy with a teddy bear. He pulled away from his embrace and walked to the bathroom. He pissed and grabbed a drink of water, rinsing the taste of Jesse's nut from his mouth. He went to the window and looked out at the early morning sky turning pink at the edges over the Three Sisters. He looked down at the parking lot, and a grandpa-looking man was loading up suitcases into an SUV. The man looked up at Eli, his mouth falling open as he saw him. The man's face looked serious for a moment, then broke into a big grin. He looked at Jesse and gave him a big thumbs-up. It was only then Eli realized he was standing naked in the window. He waved to the man and turned back to the bed. Seeing the man sent a pang of sadness through Eli. He missed his own grandfather intensely. He crawled back into bed, settling in against Jesse again, who stirred and pulled him close again. Eli turned sideways and curled his body against his new buddy. He laid his face against Jesse's and rubbed his hands lightly across the blond hairs on his chest and belly. *What the fuck am I doing,* he thought? He had no idea why, but this big blond lug felt good to him – safe and normal. *I could use a big dose of safe and normal right now.* He drifted off to sleep listening to Jesse's heartbeat, dreaming of his life before.

Chapter 2

Eli pushed his long black hair out of his eyes and felt the wind blow the small crop of dark fur under his arms against his ruddy skin. The storm was almost on him and he stood defiantly on the rock outcropping, feeling the mist from the first drops in the wind pepper his face and smooth chest. He raised his arms wide to embrace the fierce weather, daring it to do its worst. The rain came down harder now, until his hair flattened against his head and lay heavy on his neck. The beads ran down his chest to his flat belly, glistening like diamonds on the tips of his nipples and like glitter in the small ring of thick pubes that framed his penis.

"Go ahead, Gitche Manitou," the young man shouted into the howling wind. "Fuck me in the ass one more time. I can take it. You have bent me over more times than I can count. You have plowed me until your onishiwan have emptied your seed into my ass and poured down my legs. And I am still here." His fists clinched and shook in the wind as his body stood rigid and wet in the melee.

The wind howled harder and blew the boy almost off the rock, but his bare feet gripped the rock harder. The amulet around his neck bounced and spun in the storm, rubbing against the rivers of rain pouring off his chest. The leather pouch held the feathers, stones, and a tiny clay jar containing the essence of his *Nimishomis,* his grandfather. Tears streaked down his cheeks and he tasted the saltiness along with the rain. He was a man now. He had endured so much. He had celebrated the manhood ceremony with brothers of his clan, the survival skills, the spiritual vision quest in the sweat lodge, and the circumcision. But for the last five months, he had suffered so much as an orphan. He had been passed around from one foster home to the next, like a cum rag at a circle jerk. His body had been abused and scarred, though not nearly as much as his heart and self-esteem.

He had set at the feet of his *Nimishomis* since his mother had died when he was three. His grandfather had taught him the old ways, and opened his eyes to the spirit world. Sunnukkuhkau was revered in his village, honored and feared. His name meant "He who crushes," and Eli had seen first-hand exactly why. Eli's father, Makkapitew, whose name meant "He has large teeth" had died before Eli was born. But the power and curse that lived in his father's blood and seed, and in his grandfather before, now lived within him.

As a young boy, he would accompany his grandfather to the forest, to the hot springs to bathe. He watched *Nimishomis'* strong back ripple with muscles as he washed, the scars silver in the dappled light of the dark woods. Eli would stand between his grandfather's legs and allow the man to scrub his body with the cleansing powder, whispering prayers and blessings as he did. His strong hands would scour away the dirt and sweat from hours of play and farm work, sliding across his skin and rubbing it clean in the hot steamy water. Eli marveled at the size and girth of Sunnukkuhkau's penis and wondered if his own would ever look the same. Now, as he looked down at the heavy tool stretched long and low between his legs, he smiled and knew the answer. His grandfather had assured him it would be so.

"Your manhood will be powerful and mighty, like mine and your father's. Your seed is meant to carry on the glory and the curse. The right woman may come into your life, but beware of giving your seed to females who are not your mate. If you feel the burning, find a brother and share yourself with him. It will be safer and will help you manage your desires and needs."

As he grew, he wondered exactly what his grandfather's words had meant. He spent many nights wrapped in the blankets with his friend, Makuk. Their hands had explored and pleasured one another, rubbing hardness against one another and finding new ways to experience the quickening. Makuk would lay on his belly as Eli rubbed his prick in the crack of the boy's ass until he shuddered in pleasure. Then he would lie still as Makuk's penis slid back and forth in his own crack until the boy collapsed on top of him, breathing hard. Their bodies were smooth and hard and he loved the feeling of the warmth and tenderness of his friend. He and Makuk had shared the manhood ceremony when they turned eighteen years old. They were sent into the woods to live off the land for two weeks. They had been naked and totally alone, with only a knife and their wits to help them. The boys stayed still for the first night, cold, and not knowing what to do. But by the next day, they found their courage and made a fire, and trapped a rabbit. From then on, they were happy as they could be. At night, they lay in a clearing, looking up at the dazzling starscape above their heads. They would touch and fondle one another, taking turns rubbing and exploring each other's bodies. They dared one another to suck on each other's penis. In the end, they locked together in a mutual embrace, nursing on one anther until the quickening rippled through them once again. Sometime during that two weeks, the regular thrill in his belly had given way to another sensation as the warm spurt of Makuk's seed filled his mouth or hand. He had gasped as his own seed came forth, flooding his friend's mouth. And somewhere deep within, a growing growl, a snarling knot in his stomach tightened. Almost overnight, it seemed he began to sprout thick black hair around his cock and full sack. He and Makuk had laid beside one another, gripping each other's hand, as the Shaman performed the circumcision with a knife sharper than a razor. They sat in the hot springs together as their cocks healed and proudly showed a wide mushroom tip now.

One afternoon as he and Sunnukkuhkau bathed, Eli listened to his grandfather say, "You are a man now. I suppose you must now be able to make seed. Is it so with you and your *Niijii*, Makuk?"

"Yes, *Nindede* (Father)."

A weary, knowing look moved across the weathered face and he held Eli's face in his hands.

"Eluwilussit (Eli's full Ojibwa name), your name means 'Holy One.' You are gifted in ways you have yet to understand. Now that you are a man and able to make seed, the quickening will change for you. Your blood will burn on the next moon and you will feel the true change. That is your nature."

Eli stared at his grandfather, feeling the moisture flee from his mouth, as he struggled to swallow. Inside, he knew there was always something else. As he and Makuk laid together and shared their bodies and semen, he could feel it growing and manifesting in his gut. The dreams of running naked in the forest, the metallic taste of blood in his mouth, the pounding in his head, and the sensation of ripping his friend to bits for some inexplicable reason, had all been part of his dream life in the past few weeks.

"Why Papa?" Eli whispered. "What is wrong with me?"

"Nothing. You are perfect. You are holy in every way."

"But what does it mean?"

Sunnukkuhkau looked deep into the boy's eyes as he held him close. "You are a Wendigo, Eluwilussit. As was your father and as am I."

Chapter 3

Jesse's phone alarm woke the firefighters from a deep sleep. The sun was bright along the edges of the blackout curtains in the room.

"Shit, man. I was sleeping so good," Jesse said stretching his big frame across the small bed, practically knocking Eli out onto the floor. He climbed out of the covers, his round ass bouncing as he headed to the bathroom with an impressive morning wood, swinging between his legs. Eli rubbed his eyes and rolled over to look at his phone.

"Damn, look at that booty," Jesse said from the bathroom, catching the reflection of Eli's ample butt in the mirror. Eli grinned and reached back and pulled his cheeks apart, flashing his hole at Jesse. "Christ on the cross," Jesse muttered.

Eli rolled out of bed and went into the bathroom. Jesse was shaving a two or three-day scruff off his face. Eli took a loud piss into the toilet. Jesse grinned that big smile as he drug his Dollar Shave Club blade across his stubbled cheeks. "Last shave for me for a couple of weeks probably." He reached over and ran his hand over Eli's smooth face. "No shaving for you, right Sitting Bull?"

Eli rolled his eyes but smiled. "Once in a while, but not much. Not like you, Chewbacca. You are a fucking monkey."

"Hey, that's Thor the Monkey," Jesse said with another grin.

Eli flushed the toilet and turned on the shower and climbed inside. He stood under the water, letting the hot water pour over his head and wash away the dreams. He had to keep it together. These white boys were not going to understand any of his shit. Being a shifter would simply blow their minds all the way. A draft of cold air wafted through the moist air, causing Eli's nipples to harden. He opened his eyes to find Jesse standing in front of him. Jesse held one of the small hotel soaps in his hand and began to rub it across Eli's chest, and under his arms, and down his belly. Eli felt like he was seven again, bathing with his grandfather. He grabbed another tiny soap and rubbed it across Jesse's fuzzy chest, lathering up the hair, and watching the bubbles flow down his flat belly to his hard dick, surrounded by thick blond fur. Jesse's soapy fingers slide underneath Eli's sack and penetrated his ass, causing him to groan.

"I think I owe you something from last night, brother," Jesse said in a deep, early morning growl. "Assume the position, rookie," he said, spinning Eli around in the bathtub. Eli gripped the wall as Jesse moved in behind him, the head of his penis rubbing against Eli's boyhole. Jesse pulled Eli's ass apart and pushed the thick, mushroom head into Eli's soft asshole, causing the boy to grunt and exhale with a groan. Jesse's thick penis was no little boy's pecker. He had a man-sized cock that stretched Eli's hole wide, though still easily manageable compared to his Wendigo brothers. Jesse gripped his waist and began to pump in and out of his tightness in a fast rhythm that smacked and popped in the echoing shower. Jesse pulled Eli back against him, turning his head and kissing him deeply as he fucked his ass. Jesse reached around and stroked Eli's cock, which seemed once again to grow into an impossibly huge slab of meat. Jesse grunted and unloaded his balls into his new buddy's ass. With a soft groan, Eli's sperm shot out in thick, white blasts to the tiled wall.

"Holy shit, Geronimo. What's up with that dick of yours? I've never seen a cock grow that much when it's hard. Must be like a foot long."

"Nah, just seems that way because I'm kind of a small guy. You're the one with the horse cock, Thor. Thanks for clearing my sinuses this morning. Fuck!"

Jesse smiled and pulled the short man close to him and kissed him deeply. "I didn't think you and I would hit it off but I can see that was bullshit. Feels like you are just one of the gang."

"So, you think I'll fit into the crew okay?"

"Yeah. You're gonna do just fine."

An hour later, the firefighters were on the road to the Black Crater fire. Their bellies were full after a big breakfast. They drove with the windows down, toward the black column of smoke they saw in the distance in the Mount Jefferson wilderness. Jesse reached over and took Eli's hand and held it, rubbing his thumb across Eli's brown hand.

"Thanks, bro, for being so cool and shit. I kinda didn't expect all that but it really rocked. I sorta need to tell you though. Um…"

Eli laughed. The first real laugh since he had met the big guy, and it was musical and sincere. "You asshole. You have a boyfriend or girlfriend or something, right?"

"Yeah. I mean, I do. Brandon and I are kind of a thing. We play with the other guys in the crew so it's not that. He is totally fine with us fucking if we feel like it. It's just, I didn't want to give the idea that we would turn into boyfriends or something. We will be really open to having fun with you whenever, but it wouldn't be fair to let you think I was a completely free agent or something. In case that matters to you."

Eli smiled and shrugged. "Well, it kind of sucks, but then, I am just a temp guy. Didn't expect to come out here and fall in love and find my forever man. So it's all good. I'll look forward to whatever time we get together."

"Tent sex is pretty great," Jesse said with his big grin. "I mean, that's where I really lost my cherry and everything with Brandon. Since then, I've been fucked just about everywhere, out in the woods, and around a fire camp you could think of. I kind of love it."

"I couldn't tell, bro," Eli said sarcastically. He squeezed Jesse's hand and watched the high desert turn into a dense fir forest as they neared the fire.

"You got somebody back home?" Jesse asked.

"Had some. Lost them not too long ago, so not really anyone right now."

"Sorry to hear, man. You want to talk about it?"

"Nah. It's cool, man." The warm wind whipped Eli's hair around his face as the men drove in silence, further into the forest, his mind full of memories.

Chapter 4

Eli had been forbidden from sharing this revelation with Makuk or anyone else. In the next few weeks, Sunnukkuhkau told him much about the curse and glory of his family. The males in Eli's family had been Wendigo for centuries, although sometimes the curse did not manifest. It appeared to be very strong within Sunnukkuhkau and his son. It became apparent to Eli that the curse had brought about his father's death, and might very well be the reason his mother was dead as well. There was so much sorrow in his grandfather's eyes when he asked about it, Eli decided to not pursue the question. His grandfather explained what he would experience at the next full moon, and Eli counted the days with dread and wonderment. What would it mean? Sunnukkuhkau promised to be present with Eli, to help him with the transformation, and help him rein in his killer instincts.

Eli could tell something profound was building within him. As he and Makuk spent time together in the woods, they would sometimes give in again to the deep desires of their flesh. Eli felt himself growing stronger, and his desires deeper and darker. He was no longer content to share the soft touches or sucking. One week before the full moon, during one of their afternoons together, Eli felt a blackness cover his vision and he forced Makuk's legs apart and tried to penetrate him. When he came to his senses, he was filled with shame and horror with what he had done and he fled home.

Sunnukkuhkau found Eli on a tree later that evening, and pulled the boy close to him, trying to comfort him. Eli's guilt poured forth and he told his grandfather everything. The older man kissed him tenderly, and told him all would be well, and promised to make sure that Makuk was not permanently injured. For the next week, Eli saw his friend from a distance only. The boy would stare at Eli, and then run away. Eli's heart broke that he had hurt his friend and ruined their relationship. Most nights, tears would just fall down from his eyes, until he fell asleep. His heart was heavy and he was so filled with sadness, that his grandfather truly worried about the boy. But, time would have to heal this wound.

One day before the full moon, Eli woke in a startle from a deep sleep. In the dimness of his room, he sensed someone was there.

"Makuk?" Eli whispered.

"You hurt me, but I forgive you," the soft flat reply came from the corner.

"Niijii, please forgive me. I didn't mean it."

"I know. My father says the blood fever can make boys do such things?"

"What?" Eli felt his belly contract. Is it possible that Makuk knew his dark secret?

"The blood fever. You know, boners and wanting to fuck and stuff."

Eli smiled. "Yeah, that's it for sure. You just get my blood fever going, brother."

Makuk moved closer to his bed. The boy was naked and his penis was rigid against his flat belly. "I think it's my turn," the boy said in a whisper.

Eli sank to his knees and took his friend into his mouth and then laid across his bed, his legs spread wide. Makuk found his hole, and pushed roughly inside as Eli gasped. The boy rode him hard and long until both were wet with sweat. Eli felt Makuk shudder and fall against his back, spent and breathing hard.

"Did you like it? Did it hurt?"

Eli pulled the boy close. "Yes to both. Now we are even, brother." Makuk slid in beside him under the covers and snuggled close, his face resting against Eli's.

"Um, I'm going to go on a trip tomorrow, Makuk. I might be gone for a while."

"What kind of a trip, Eli? Can I come, too?"

"Not this time, Niijii. It is a quest with Sunnukkuhkau. It is about my father and I am supposed to learn great things. I will tell you about it soon. We are more than friends, Niijii. We are *Niishime* (brothers)."

"I love you, Eli."

"I love you, too, Makuk. We are bonded with our seed now. We have bred one another."

"I like it. I hope we can keep doing it."

Eli hugged the boy tightly and fell asleep feeling, his heart beat alongside his friend.

Chapter 5

Eli and his grandfather left early the next morning. The boy reluctantly left the warmth and comfort of his bed and his friend, and moved silently alongside Sunnukkuhkau. Mist hugged the pines and spruce trees that stood as silent sentinels on the forest trail. Eli felt the dampness hug his body and chill him to the bone, but he kept a close pace behind his grandfather, stopping only to drink from a stream or empty his bladder along with *Nimishomis,* their sparkling straw-colored arcs of piss loud and musical in the early morning quiet. The man and boy traveled most of the day, finally arriving at a rock outcropping that overlooked Lake Superior, *Gitche Gumee.* The sun glinted on the water like an ocean of sapphires. The sandstone ledge was warm and inviting. Eli watched his grandfather strip naked and lay on the warm stone, his clothing in a pillow behind his head. Eli followed his lead and felt the sun glow behind his closed eyelids like a fire. The warm breeze teased the soft hairs under his arms and around his half-erect penis. He wanted to pleasure himself, but kept still, letting the sound of the wind fill his ears, and the sun warm his brown skin until sweat popped out on his forehead and upper lip. He tasted the salty drops as he licked his lips, and ran his tongue far above his lip to the soft black fur that had started its growth on his upper lip.

Eli must have dozed off earlier, and his grandfather woke him up to fulfill an important task – to fill a small clay pot with his seed. He did not understand what it was for, but he did it anyway, away from his grandfather's sight. After a while, he gave the clay pot to his grandfather, and the man rose and went to a small spring that bubbled on the face of the rock outcropping, and filled the pot with the clear water until it was full.

"This will be important later, Eluwilussit. Tonight, you truly become the man the Great Spirit has created you to be. You will need to trust and believe. As the full moon rises, you will transform and shift into your Wendigo form. It will be painful and glorious. I will be here to guide you as I will transform as well. Here, eat this. The sun is setting, and I will need to restrain you until you are more used to the change."

Eli's mind was spinning as he gobbled down the elk jerky and dried cherries. He ate some flatbread and walnuts, drinking a sour wine-tasting drink from a flask. It numbed his mouth somewhat and felt warm to his belly and all the way to his balls. In fact, by the time he finished his meal and drink, his penis was rock hard and flat against his belly. He tried to hide his erection behind his hand but it was hopeless.

"It is the mead. Warriors often use it when they are ready to mount a bride or brother. It will remain for some time," his grandfather said. "Every erection is a miracle from the Great Spirit. Never be ashamed of your hard cock. It is a gift and celebration of your manhood."

He watched his grandfather's strong, muscled body unpack leather straps with fur cuffs of some kind attached. He fastened these tightly to iron rings fastened to the rock wall behind them. The sandstone began to glow orange, and then to bloody red, as the sun disappeared over *Gitche Gumee.* The air grew colder but his face and body seemed to radiate a vibrant heat. His cock was still hard and leaking, and his breathing had begun to be harder and his pulse quickened. Fear gripped his heart.

His grandfather took him in his arms and held him tight. "The shifting is about to start, Eluwilussit. Come with me. Try not to fear. Embrace your manhood and your power. I am here to guide you. You will soon run with me and become one with your true self." Eli's grandfather gently led him to the rock wall and fastened the fur-covered leather straps to the boy's wrists, ankles, and waist. Eli's heart banged a throbbing tattoo against his chest as he watched the sky turn purple, and then dissolve into a glittering black starfield. Eli's mouth was dry. His breathing was now coming in hard gasps. His hands were straining against the bands, his fingers rigid like claws. His legs trembled and his ears were so full of his own heartbeat, he thought his eardrums would burst. He felt his grandfather's warm hand press against his belly.

"Watch the moon rise, Eluwilussit. Your time is near."

As the moon shimmered in the inky sky, turning the dark water to silver, Eli's head slammed back against the rock, and his body spasmed into a rictus of pain, his arms and legs tearing against the bindings. Eli opened his mouth and screamed, deep and guttural from somewhere beyond any voice he had ever heard before. His throat ripped open with the howl that began as a high-pitched shriek, and descended to a low, rumbling snarl. The still air was filled with the crack of bones and tendons as Eli's face elongated into a drooling muzzle of foam and froth. His fingers popped and his nails sliced forward into four-inch knives. His back arched, and fur sprouted from his armpits, chest, belly, balls and ass, and wrapped like a blanket around his trembling form. He lost control of his bladder and his piss sprayed hard on his chest and belly, and dripped from his furry genitals that now grew to a massive foot-long penis, thick and throbbing. His scrotum filled with egg-sized testicles and lay heavy and low between his muscled hairy legs. The roar ripped through his throat again and razor-like fangs grew from his incisors.

Eli took a deep breath, and his nose filled with the most intoxicating aromas of his life. He sniffed again and took in the scent of his grandfather. He smelled piss and semen, sweat, and remnants of food. He could smell rabbits, birds, deer, and so much more. He opened his eyes and stared at the image in front of him. His grandfather, or what should have been his grandfather, stood before him. He was seven feet tall with a rack of antlers sprouting from his head, heavy and dangerous. He was covered in fur. Talon-like claws adorned his hands. His face was stretched into a muzzle filled with huge fangs, dripping with saliva. His nostrils flared, blood-red eyes stared into his. A huge horse-like cock fell between his legs, impossibly long and heavy. As his grandfather gripped Eli's face with his hands, Eli suddenly was connected with him in a primal, non-verbal link. His grandfather opened his mouth and snarled. He sniffed Eli's face, belly, and groin, and howled in an ear-splitting growl. Eli looked at the leather bands holding him and broke them as if they were Red Vines. He stood before his transformed grandfather, who licked his face with a hot, wet tongue before bounding away, Eli close at his heels.

The two tore through the forest. Eli's senses were almost on fire they were so acute. Within minutes, he had found a rabbit and seized it. He tore the animal in half and drank its blood, and feasted on its flesh and fat. He fled after his grandfather and locked on to the new scent. Their telepathy connected and the two began to chase, and then flank until the deer stumbled into both of them in a clearing. Eli flung himself onto the animal and tore its head from its body in one wrenching slice of jaws and claws. Minutes later, Eli stood drench in blood and flesh, his belly full and satiated. His ears and nose picked up a new scent, and he flew off in a new direction. His grandfather barked a warning, but Eli ignored it and flew toward the new olfactory delight.

Chapter 6

Two miles away, Rod Chambers and his best buddy, Craig Holly, had turned in for the night. The men usually got away and into the woods once every month or so. The pretense was fairly ironclad. Their wives were certainly not interested in grubby, primitive camping, with no toilet or showers. It was the perfect ruse and the men had been enjoying the stolen weekends for more than three years now. They had discovered sex together as boys on campouts exactly like these, with other scouts or leaders obliviously snoring away in tents next to theirs. They had found they shared a common interest and curiosity that had grown into a full-blown love affair by the time they were seniors. But as life often does, they found themselves also drawn to girls and a more predictable life. As they grew a bit older, they lost touch with one another and spent the next ten years or so being family men and fucking their wives, filling their bellies with babies three times each.

Then, just a little over three years ago, they ran into one another at a Pop Warner football games for their oldest sons. For Rod, it felt like he had found a missing part of his heart. For Craig, it was like the past ten years had hardly happened. The men sat in the bleachers, catching up with one another, their legs pressed against one another, totally uncharacteristic of their interactions with most other men. Late in the third quarter, they made a trip to the men's room, pulling up to the urinal trough next to one another. Rod felt his cock swell as he pulled it out to piss alongside his school buddy. They stood in silence, watching the urine splash into the grimy porcelain. Long after they finished, they stood there, arms touching at the elbows, slowly stroking their dicks until they were hard and dripping with pre-cum. It took every bit of their self-control to not lock themselves in a stall and start sucking. With no one still around, Rod pulled out his phone and snapped photos of their hard dicks touching one another.

They returned to the game and traded cell numbers. Rod texted the photo to Craig who adjusted his dick as he sat in the stands, discretely looking at the photo under his jacket. The following weekend, the men had found themselves in the woods in a small dome tent. They had spent the weekend naked and making up for lost time. They had fucked five times, sucked one another more times than they could count. It was a glorious reunion. They hiked naked to some nearby hot springs and made love on the bank of the pool. A couple of college boys ended up walking in on them but they didn't care. In the end, the boys were more than happy to get their dicks sucked by the brazen dads, who hungrily lapped up the loads of the surprised hikers.

The men had continued their relationship now for the past three years, sneaking away as often as possible. Sometimes they brought their boys along, and ended up waiting for the kids to fall asleep in their tent before retreating to their own, to quietly bang one another while the boys snored next door. Quite a few times, they had invited other men to join them and more often than not, they ended up balls deep in the guests or else riding their poles, or blowing each other until they were spent.

Chapter 7

Silently, Eli lay on his belly in the undergrowth. He could see the heat signatures of the men fifty feet in front of him. His mouth watered as the intoxicating smell of sweat, semen, and ass filled his muzzle. His cock swelled to its full length and girth and he rutted against the moss-covered ground. He could still hear his grandfather's warning barks in the distance, but Eli ignored them. He was coming close, he would be on him soon. He sprang forward in a blur.

With a blinding crash, a whirlwind of fur and claws slashed the dome tent to shreds. Craig saw the horrifying creature for a second before feeling the razor sharp claws clamp around his butt and hurl him into a nearby spruce, knocking him unconscious. Rod, who had been flattened by the attack, gasped to regain his breath as he felt himself pulled up again to his knees. The steamy breath of the being burned across the back of his head and face, saliva dripped down his neck and back. In a flash, he was impaled by the creature's cock. All twelve inches of thick animal meat entered Rod's anus and pinned him to the ground. The man's howl of pain was cut short as the blow to his head rendered him unconscious. Eli gripped the man's lifeless form by the waist, and he slammed his monstrous cock deeper and deeper into Rod's ruined manhole until he cried out in a large growling bark, unloading his thick seed into the man's bowels.

Now that he had bred the man, he raised his claws to sever his head, and feast on his warm blood when a thunderous blow slammed into his body, knocking the boy creature ten feet in the air, landing with a crash in the remnants of the tent. Eli spun to attack only to find himself face-to-face with Sunnukkuhkau.

"No! Eli stop. You must not!" he shouted, gripping the creature with his hands. Eli raised his hands to claw his grandfather when the man's hand darted forward and slapped the boy across his muzzle, then reached below to grip his balls in a vise-like grip. Eli's grandfather squeezed and twisted the boy's testicles until he fell to his knees in a heap.

"Drink this," Sunnukkuhkau ordered, tipping the contents of the clay bowl into Eli's mouth. The semen-flavored water was hot and strong, but as it moved down his throat, the blood fever broke and Eli collapsed on the ground. The boy began to transform again, shifting back to his human form. As he did, Eli's mind filled with the realization of what had just happened. He rose and tore away from his grandfather, running headlong into the night, tears blinding him. In a mile, he stopped and bent forward, vomiting into the ferns on the side of the path. He collapsed to the ground. Sunnukkuhkau caught him and picked him up in his arms, carrying him like a baby back to men's campground. Eli lay motionless on the ground as Sunnukkuhkau ministered to the men, pouring some liquid into their mouths and muttering incantations over them. He finished helping the men recover, leaving them unconscious and breathing. He lifted Eli into his arms again and took off at a fast jog back to their campsite. When they arrived, he gently laid Eli on the blankets they had brought and flopped down beside him, his chest heaving. The two men fell into a deep, sudden sleep.

As he slept, Eli dreamed he was the Wendigo again, running wild and free. He hunted animals and feasted on their flesh and blood. He dreamed of Makuk. In the vision, he held the boy down and penetrated him violently with his massive penis and in the end, he attacked him.

Eli awoke with a scream. Sunnukkuhkau grabbed for the boy and took him into his arms, rocking him back and forth.

"Shhh, Eli. It is only a dream. You did not hurt the men too badly, thank goodness. But you must take care. It is in your nature to kill men, but we must learn to control that. It is in your nature to ravish those you lust after as well, but great care must be taken in such a *way as not to damage or hurt them. The blood fever will always cause your lust a* powerful way. I will teach you how to keep the urges under enough control not to hurt or kill humans or some animals."

Eli looked up at his grandfather with red eyes. His throat still ached from the howling and screams. "Did I kill those men? I… I raped that man badly," he said, choking back sobs.

"I made sure they will be fine. They will have many bruises and quite the story to tell. And I dare say they may even have a deep hunger and craving for mating. That is what happens when a Wendigo penetrates a man or woman. Their sexual desires become greatly heightened. You did no permanent damage, though yes, you would have killed the man had I not stopped you. I will show you how to control the blood fever where you will not go too far. But for a boy Wendigo, this is a hard lesson. Trust me, Eli. Your father and I knew all too well what it was like to have the blood fever boil hot within us. Your father almost killed several men and women until he learned to control his urge. When I was a boy, I am sad to say I did not have such a mentor."

Eli looked at his grandfather and saw the sorrow and pain in his eyes. "Did you hurt someone badly, Papa?"

"Yes. The first night I shifted, I killed a man and his son who were hunting in the woods. I raped them and… did something to them. I almost took my own life. I was so devastated. Luckily, our shaman found me and made it his goal to help teach me the ways of Wendigo, even though he was not one himself. I almost killed him several times. It was a desperate time for me and one I hope to make much better for you. Follow my instructions well, Eli. You will be a strong, powerful man with a great gift."

Eli hugged his grandfather tight and felt their hearts beat together as one. Over the next year, the lessons continued on each full moon. There were several close calls in which Eli came close to killing an innocent bystander that just happened to be in the wrong place at the wrong time. Eli was introduced to two other Wendigo boys from neighboring villages, all of whom were being mentored by Sunnukkuhkau. After the first three moons, Eli's grandfather took boys to the woods on each full moon and taught them to hunt more discretely, to channel their passions and bloodlust more carefully, and to rein in their power somewhat. The most important safety mechanism was the *niinag,* which was the Algonquin word for penis. It was a smooth brass dildo that contained a solution of blood, Wendigo saliva and semen, and *manoomin* (wild rice). The *niinag* was inserted rectally before shifting. If the blood fever raised the body temperature to 103°, which normally happened when a Wendigo was in the midst of a particularly violent *mazhi* (intercourse), or preparing to attack a human, the cylinder would automatically inject the solution which rendered the Wendigo impotent and nauseous enough to quell the attack. Interestingly, the body temperature did not increase to this level when hunting game or participating in intercourse with other Wendigo or a willing partner.

So Eli and his new Wendigo brothers, Sami and Reyn, sat at the feet of Sunnukkuhkau and learned as much as they could. They listened intently as the shaman taught them how to prepare the mixture and put into the *niinag*. They giggled and groaned as they slid the smooth cylinders into their respective assholes until they rested against their prostate, learning to manage the new sensation of walking around with a fat rod in their anus. Soon, the boys learned that the movement of the *niinag* mostly made them horny... all the time. The boys walked around in a constant state of arousal when they wore the *niinag*. They only needed to wear it a day or so before the full moon, but they took to wearing much of the time, enjoying the constant pressure and excitement that kept them half erect.

Chapter 8

"Hey wake up, sleepy. We are here," Jesse said, punching Eli on the shoulder. "Man, you must have really been dreaming. Look at that thing again," Jesse said reaching over to grip Eli's erection through his Nomex. Eli pushed his hand away, he needed to piss badly. He shifted in his seat and felt the smooth pressure of the *niinag* pushing against his prostate. He had inserted it when he had moment while Jesse had checked out of the room. He wondered if he should not use it, but feared to be without it in this strange and clearly tempting environment. The full blood fever would be on him in two days and he would have to shift and run the woods at night. He could just imagine what Sunnukkuhkau would say about this situation. He clambered out of the pickup and grabbed his gear, and headed off with Jesse to find the rest of the crew. Eli had to jog to keep up with Jesse's long strides, but running came naturally to him. He headed from the parking lot into the school where the fire camp was set up.

"Go ahead and check in here. Show them your red card and all that. I'm going to go find Brandon, and I'll be back before you head off to fire cache to get your gear," Jesse said.

"Okay," Eli said, taking his wallet out and looking for his red card. He walked up to the check in desk where a young Latina girl was sitting behind a computer, clacking away on the keyboard.

"Um, Hi. Eli Bungo, here to check in. AD Firefighter joining Hart Mountain Hotshots."

The girl looked up. "Hi. Did you say, Bunko?"

Eli groaned inwardly. *So tired of this*, he thought. "No, Bungo… B-U-N-G-O."

"Oh, sorry. Um, do you have a resource order?" the girl asked with a smile.

"Yeah, hold on." Eli rummaged through the big pockets on the side of his pants, and bought out a folded piece of paper. "Looks like I'm C-115.21."

"Oh, here you are," she said clacking more on the computer. "Can I see your red card?"

Eli handed it to the girl who looked up at him with an even bigger smile. Their hands casually touched. Eli could instantly tell her pheromones were pumping. Her pulse quickened and he could smell her increased desire, wafting up from her tight fire pants. His own penis stiffened, making a noticeable lump in his pants. He tried to casually shift his dick into a more discreet position but felt the girl's eyes following as his hand touched his groin. She parted her lips and handed the card back to him.

"Okay, you're all done here. You will need to check in with finance and fire cache."

"Thanks," he said, giving the girl one last look before gathering up his gear to head off to finance. He saw her nipples straining hard against her t-shirt. *Man, these girls are so easy*, he thought. *I could fuck my way through this camp. I should probably give it a try one of these days pretty soon.* Eli turned in his travel CTR to finance and got the information on how to code his shift ticket to the fire. He followed the older lady's directions and headed to fire cache to check out a tent, sleeping bag and other essentials. He was standing in a line of other new arrivals when he felt a hand on his shoulder, followed by another hand on his ass. He turned to see a small guy about his height with brown curly hair and big dopey eyes and a smart ass grin. He turned the other way and saw Jesse standing beside him, his hand goosing his ass with a pinch.

"Hey, Chief Joseph," Jesse said. "This is Brandon. You know, the guy I told you about," he said, clueless. Eli just stared.

"I hope you have already learned to ignore this asshole," Brandon said, with another grin. He clapped Eli on the shoulder. "Welcome to the suck, buddy. Glad you can help us. Sounds like you are gonna fit in nicely." Leaning close to his ear, Brandon finished in a whisper. "Like you did in my boyfriend's ass," he said, with a knowing look that was somewhere between glee and fury. Eli opened his mouth to answer, but Brandon just patted him on the side of the head. "It's cool, brother. This bitch of mine can't keep his dick to himself for five minutes," he whispered. "From what I hear, I definitely have some things to look forward to getting to work with you."

Eli smiled and looked around. None of the other men in the line seemed to be paying the least bit of attention. He checked out his gear and followed Brandon and Jesse around to a corridor into the school and went inside. The air was cool and comfortable, a huge transistion from the smoky heat outside.

"Aren't I suppose to put my tent up outside?" he asked. He saw the ocean of tents surrounding the school in all directions.

"Now that we are going on night shift, we get to sleep in the school, so it will be dark while we sleep during the day. So, we can set our tents up in the classrooms. But pretty much, we just sleep in a big group in the room so we don't have to worry about the tent setup and everything. It's cooler and nicer. Come on, we are just down here," Brandon said.

Eli followed the short guy, noticing that he was staring at the young guy's ass that filled out his Nomex very nicely, like Jesse. *Damn, these white boys have some butt on them for sure compared to most,* he thought. He could smell the warm, wet crotches in their pants, as well as the faint musk from their armpits and asses. *These two were a veritable buffet of scent*, he thought. When Brandon opened the door, Eli was practically bowled over from the olfactory overload.

The room was packed with men. Every orifice in the room seemed to be screaming in Eli's nose. He was almost knocked over by the scent of sweat, moist balls, ass, old piss and cum. Eli's dick instantly became hard and he knew there was no way these guys weren't going to see. Brandon took him over to a large man with reddish brown hair and trimmed goatee.

"Hey, Jake, here's your new AD. This is Eli Bunghole," Brandon said with a flourish.

Jake scowled at Brandon and pushed passed him to take Eli's hand. "Welcome, Eli. Pay no attention to this jackass."

"Hey!" Brandon said offended.

"Fuck off," Jake said quietly but sternly. One big smell let Eli know there was no doubt who the alpha of this pack was. The heat and pheromones emanating from Jake were powerful and utterly male. Eli could smell the pee staining his shorts and it was like perfume, heady and robust. "Really glad you could drop everything and come help us out. We hated to lose Big, but his family was having a medical crisis and he needed to be there."

"Hope it wasn't too serious," Eli said.

"His grandfather had a heart attack and he was Big's father for the most part of his life. It doesn't look good so he needed to be there."

"Man. Sorry to hear. I know all about that."

"That sucks, buddy. So, did Jesse take care of you last night?" The loaded question sat there like a giant fart in the busy room. Jake stared straight at Eli, clearly waiting to hear his reply.

"Actually, I think I took care of him pretty good."

"Now that's something I'd like to hear all about sometime soon," Jake said with a grin. He leaned forward and whispered. "I could see your fucking dick all the way across the room when you came in. Nice tool, man."

Eli blushed. "Thanks, I guess. I'm always getting a boner at inappropriate times."

Jake shook his head. "No such thing, brother. Every erection is a miracle."

Eli laughed. "That sounds like something my grandfather would have said."

"Smart man, no doubt. Okay, well, get settled and we will be taking off to evening briefing. Glad you're here, Eli. You're gonna fit in just fine," Jake said, patting Eli on the ass.

Brandon came back over and grabbed Eli's gear. "Come on over here, man." The small firefighter weaved his way through a minefield of air mattresses and sleeping bags. "There's a free spot over here. You can either have that single bed air mattress there or double up with Bayard. He has a queen airbed, but he doesn't mind sharing." Eli noticed most of the area was filled up with queen airbeds with two sleeping bags on them. Here and there were some single beds, but even those seemed to be pushed together with another.

"You guys really like snuging up."

"Yeah, just a bunch of gay boys on a campout for the most part," Brandon said, matter of factly. "You okay with that, right?"

"Yeah, I guess."

"Sounded like you were cool last night."

"Hotel room is a different scene than this, but it's all good. I'll just follow everyone's lead."

"Then, you're gonna be cock deep in an ass sometime early tomorrow morning." Brandon said, with a giggle.

"So, who's this Bayard guy?"

"That's him right over there, the guy in the yellow shirt."

"Funny," Eli said, looking at the twenty guys in the room, all wearing yellow fire shirts.

"See that guy over there with the beard and the red bandana on? That's him."

Eli stared. Even from here when he concentrated, he could smell the musky crotch and armpits of the man. The smell of marijuana smoke and semen completed the heady scent along with a small tang of urine. Another deep sniff and Eli detected he was. Eli's heightened senses could tell he was a gentle, kind man with a bit heart, and a big hunger for cock. Eli put his gear down on the other side of the queen airbed.

"Looks like it's Bayard's lucky day for sure," Brandon said. "Hope you are interested in checking out more dick than just his."

Eli smiled. As he walked by Brandon he reached out and gripped the small man's basket. "That's a distinct possibility, brother."

Chapter 9

Eli moved through the thick smoke along with the rest the hotshots as they worked on a burnout on the western flank of the fire. It was slow going, hard work. More than once, as they moved through the tall brush, Eli felt a thick Western rattlesnake slither over his boots, in an effort to outrun the fire that was pushing him out of his home. Eli worked with Jesse on one side of him and another big blond lunkhead named Colton on the other. Even through the acrid burn, Eli could smell the pheromones oozing from the men, especially Colton. When the big man had stopped digging fire line and pulled out his fat cock to take a piss, the odor of his groin filled Eli's nostrils like a dog in heat. The man absolutely exuded maleness, piss, and desire. Eli knew this type of animal. This one rutted with the best of them. He fucked hard and long and loved his dick in a man's ass more than anything. As he looked up through the smoky night sky, Eli could just make out the outline of an almost full moon. Tomorrow, he would shift whether he wanted to or not. He kept wondering how in the hell he was going to manage it. As the monotony of the work continued, his mind filled with images from his past.

Eli had been surprised a week after his bonding experience with his friends to find Makuk standing at his door. He and his friend had sadly grown apart with his new focus on his Wendigo brethren and learning to shift and the joys of that. He had promised to tell Makuk his secret, but now felt that was foolish. How could an ordinary boy understand? He had been friendly with Makuk at school and tried as well as he could to spend time with him. But as the weeks had turned to months, the boys had less and less in common. Makuk seemed young and silly to Eli, compared to Sami and Reyn. Twice in the past year, they had spent the night together. Makuk was eager to rekindle the boyhood love the two had shared. Eli reluctantly agreed, worried that he would lose control again. Makuk was dumbfounded with how Eli had grown. His penis was a thick, heavy man-sized member now, surrounded with thick black hair and low-hanging balls. Makuk's penis was still short and his balls had only just dropped.

when a blinding slap caught him on the side of the head. When he turned, he saw Sunnukkuhkau there, in full shifted form, ready to attack. Eli stepped back and shifted back into his human form. The older man gripped Eli by the neck and shook him violently as if he were a puppet, and his teeth rattled in his head. Eli was thrown to the ground. Sunnukkuhkau stood over him, naked and panting, anger boiling from his eyes.

"How dare you defy me? I told you to never reveal yourself to Makuk. He cannot handle it." He pointed to the small boy rolled in a ball, rocking back and forth in a fetal position.

"I... just... He wouldn't believe me!"

"Of course not, you fool! Leave now, and I will try and save us both." Sunnukkuhkau demanded.

Later that night, Eli lay in his bed, furious and sobbing. He heard his grandfather come into the room and sit on the edge of his bed. He did not turn over.

"I am sorry, Eli, but that was a grave mistake tonight. I pray that it will not come back to haunt us both. Knowledge is power, son. Your friend is weak and cannot handle this truth. I know he baited you into showing yourself, but you must never fall into that trap again. Do you understand?"

"Yes." Eli hissed under his breath. He turned fiercely to Sunnukkuhkau and glared at him. "He deserved it. I wish you hadn't stopped me."

"If I had not, you would be utterly destroyed. You would have killed your friend and your soul in the doing."

"Leave me alone, Sunnukkuhkau."

The man bent forward and kissed the salty wetness of Eli's cheek and left.

Chapter 10

"Hey, new guy. Bunghole!" a voice sounded through the dirty night air. Eli looked up and saw Colton was motioning him over.

"Dude, I was calling you for a whole minute. You have to pay more attention than that. It could get you or me killed."

"You're right. Sorry. What did you need?"

"We are taking a short break. I wondered if you wanted to suck my dick."

"What?"

"I'm just busting your balls, dude. We are taking a break, though. Come on over here and sit down before you fall down."

In all honesty, Eli wasn't the faintest bit tired. His muscles and senses were tight and alert. He smelled smoke and sexual frustration in every direction. More than a dozen men were urinating right now. At least one was taking a shit. He couldn't be sure, but he thought he might even smell semen. *Who would be rutting out here in this burn,* he thought.

"So, you're an Indian, huh? You have like a spirit animal and all that stuff," Colton said chewing on a stick of beef jerky.

Eli stared at the man and was filled with annoyance. He faced questions like this all the time. He sensed that this fool was not trying to goad him or belittle his beliefs. This one was simply too stupid to know he was being offensive. And holy shit, the scent of him was off the fucking chart. Sitting there on a mid-sized rock, his legs spread wide. The musk from his crotch was like a blast of funk into Eli's nostrils. It was all he could do not to shift and butt fuck this redneck into the middle of next week. He could taste the sweat and dampness of his nutsack in his mouth.

"Spirit guides are sacred. We usually don't discuss them."

"Hey, no offense meant. Everything is sacred to you guys. You take a dump and it's a holy site or something," Colton said with a full mouth.

Eli laughed. "Yeah. You should see the shrine around my cum rags. It's a fucking temple."

Now it was Colton's turn to laugh. A big, deep laugh all the way down to his gut. "That's funny shit, dude. So you know about all us? You cool with our particular brand of crazy."

"Yeah. Jesse kind of gave me a sneak peek last night."

"I bet he did. That boy is more horned up than me, and that's pretty damn bad."

Eli noticed the flash of the silver band on Colton's finger. "You a married guy huh? You got kids?"

Colton looked down at his blackened hands. "Nope, not yet. We hope to get a boy or two one of these days. Ben wasn't into the idea at first, but he's coming around."

Eli nodded. "That's good. How long have you been together?"

"Not that long, couple of years. Fuck, I didn't really know I was gay much before that. Benny kind of took care of that. How about you? You just like the peen or does your tomahawk swing both ways."

Eli shook his head and chuckled. These white boys had no boundaries at all, it seemed. "I haven't ever fucked a girl. But I'm not against the idea or anything."

"Fair enough. Your cock get hard when you look at pussy porn?"

"My cock gets hard eating spaghetti."

Colton roared. "A man after my own heart. Well, there's plenty of guys like pussy in our crew. And some of them like taking a bone in the butt more than the queers. Takes all kinds I guess." Colton took a big drink of water, emptying the canteen in one long gulp that trickled from his thick lips and down his trimmed goatee and onto his yellow Nomex. He burped loudly and lifted his ass off the rock and ripped off a fart that echoed in the darkness. "Time to drain the weasel and then back to work. Come on, Chief. Let's go tinkle."

Eli shook his head but followed Colton over to the edge of the black they were working on. The moonlight had turned the clearing silver. The wind had picked up so there were errant embers like fireflies dancing in the cooling air. The night glowed with a moon clearly mocking Eli and reminding him that this time tomorrow, he would shift whether he wanted to or not. His belly rumbled and his hands shook as he followed the gigantic blond cowboy into the brush. Colton stopped and unzipped his pants. He fished out his cock and balls and let it flop big and heavy on the smooth sack. He put his hands on his waist and farted again, sending a thick hot stream of clear yellow pee into the dusty ground in a big arc. Eli's nose filled with the scent, causing his penis to swell and begin to leak. He pulled his junk out and sent his hot stream in a blast toward Colton's piss.

"Goddamn, Chief. That is a huge totem pole. Did you get that big boy up Jesse's pucker last night?"

"Yes sir. He was howling at the moon."

"Fuck me. I bet he was. Damn."

"There's plenty to go around, Gomer," Eli said, waggling his erection. "You want it in your mouth or your nice round ass?"

"You got quite a mouth on you, rookie. Maybe I should fill it up with my cock."

"You can try, brother," Eli said with a grin that didn't look like a grin at all.

Colton stared at him for a while, holding his penis and shaking off errant drops. "Dude, you need to chill. I'm just messing with you."

"Me too, brother," Eli said, shaking his own boner before tucking it away. "Back to work, huh?"

"Yeah. Guess so. I'm going to go ahead and follow this line down the draw. You stay up here along the top and then go down that flank on the far west side."

"Ten-four." Eli picked up his Pulaski and moved around to the far edge of the ridge and began looking for hotspots. He turned and saw Colton carefully moving down the draw. The scent of his taint was still in Eli's nose. A low rumble purred in Eli's throat. He looked up at the moon again. He moved quickly into a stand of fir that had not been touched by the fire. He unlaced his boots and a moment later, he stood naked in the silver light. He arched his back and felt the crack and pop of his bones and joints as he shifted into his full Wendigo form. The air sizzled around him. He reached around and gave the cylinder in his ass a firm tap. It pushed against his prostate and his erection flared again. Like a silent wind, he was off.

He ran noiselessly through the forest. He bounded over boulders and over downed trees. He smelled the firefighters in the woods ahead of him. He moved close to them, avoiding exposing himself. As he flew by, heads would turn. Twice, he crept close enough and his long clawed fingers traced the crack of an ass in dirty, sweaty pants. The men would reach around to see if a blackberry vine had caught them. He moved past them like a ghost, slowly rubbing their crotches or bellies and was gone before they could see what had happened. Eli felt alive and mighty. He liked these men. His bloodlust burned hard. He needed to breed.

He turned and moved back up the hillside in a quiet blur. His eyes were sharp and perfect. He saw the heat signatures of all the men. His nose locked onto a familiar scent and he honed in on it like a lion on a kill. As he crept along the brush, he spied Colton. The man's Pulaski rested against a tree. The firefighter had his pants down around his ankles while he stroked his cock, and tugged on his big sack. He would reach up under his shirt to tweak his nipples as he stroked. Thin ribbons of pre-cum leaked from the tip of Colton's impressive penis.

In a flash of dim light, Eli appeared from the smoke as Colton stroked his dick. He came from the side and was almost on him before Colton realized something was there. Colton's eyes opened wide but he couldn't take in what he was seeing. Eli stood before him as a full Wendigo. A wide rack of antlers sprouted from his head. His face was elongated and wolf-like. His chest and belly were covered with hair. His arms were long and terribly muscled, with long razor-like talons. A massive horse cock rose between his legs on top of a sack filled with balls the size of lemons. His legs were furry and huge.

Colton was paralyzed. He turned to run but his legs were jelly. Eli gripped the man's throat and lifted him from the ground, a low rumble rolling from his jaws. His hot, wet tongue slid out and licked Colton's face until it dripped with saliva. Eli used his other hand, sliding his talons back into his fingers and gripped Colton's penis, rubbing the pre-cum off the tip and tasting the drop of honey.

"Suck me," Eli barked in a voice somewhere between a man's and beast. Colton's eyes practically popped out of his head. "Now," Eli ordered, as he lowered Colton to the ground.

With trembling hands, Colton gripped Eli's huge cock and stared at it. It drooled pre-cum like a leaky faucet. Eli's hand gripped Colton's head and pushed it onto the cock. Colton gagged and spluttered but began to fellate the creature, even beginning to establish a rhythm as the beast thrust. Only half the cock slid into Colton's mouth. The man continued to gag and retch, sending great gouts of spit into the dirt. Colton reached around and gripped the creature's round meaty ass, and drove his face again and again into the thing's crotch.

Finally, Eli pulled away and stood before Colton like a god, with the firefighter still on his knees. "Lose the boots and pants." Eli ordered in a soft bark. Colton rose and did as he was ordered, standing like a little boy who had just wet his pants at school. Eli took his unshifted hand and spun the man around.

"Grip the rock," Eli ordered. As Colton bend over, his sack hung low between his furry legs and Eli's nose and tongue licked and probed his scrotum and licked deep inside the man's asshole, pulling the muscled cheeks apart, and eating his manhole like the wild thing he was. Colton was groaning and gurgling like a man strangling. A river of saliva hung in Colton's crack and streamed from his balls and hole. Eli moved in behind him

"Don't... please!" Colton whispered.

Eli wrapped his hand around the man's face and slid seven inches of Wendigo cock into Colton's lubed hole. Eli's thick hand muffled the man's screams. Eli slid the other claws back into his fingers and gripped Colton's waist, and began to plow in and out with a fast rhythm. Tears streamed from Colton's eyes as Eli fucked deeper and deeper into the man's bowels. Eli concentrated and felt his penis shrink back in size somewhat until his furry belly rested against the man's ass. He pumped hard in and out of the stretched hole, his sack slamming into Colton's balls. Little by little, Eli sent new power to his cock, stretching the hole, and sliding even further inside the man. In a minute, Colton gripped the rock and was pushing his ass back, again and again on the fist-sized cock. Eli felt the familiar boiling in his balls. The breeding was on him.

He raised his face and roared. His semen shot like water from a fire hose deep into Colton's wrecked anus. Blast after blast of white cream filled the man's ass until it leaked out and fell to the duff-covered forest floor in great pearls. Colton cried out and his own cock erupted with four big jets of spunk, painting the red surface of the boulder. Eli pulled out, his cock making a slurping pop, as it exited Colton's ass. Eli bent and lapped at the man's crack and his seed before turning and disappearing into the darkness, leaving Colton in a heap on top of the rock.

A few minutes later, Eli reappeared, this time dressed in his fire clothes. He ran over to Colton who was still laying half naked, sprawled on the rock. The man's anus was still gaped open, a thin stream of white cream leaked from the wounded hole. Eli bent down and gathered the huge man into his arms and looked around. He saw a grove of alder to the east and took off at a fast jog, with Colton gripping around his neck. He tenderly laid the man down on the forest floor and held him tight to his chest. He listened to Colton's chest and heard his heart strong and true. Eli laid the man down and ran back to gather up his pants and boots before running back. He sat beside him and gathered the man into his arms again. There were tears in Eli's eyes now. As he nuzzled close to Colton's cheek, he could smell the man again, his fear subsided, his desire quenched. He smelled of sweat and sperm and ass. Eli gripped him tight. Finally, Colton's hand moved up to touch Eli's face.

"Did you see it?"

"Did I see what?"

"I just got raped by Bigfoot."

Chapter 11

Eli listened to Colton recounting the attack, with a mixture of horror and delight. Rarely had he enjoyed a breeding like that one. Everything about this redneck excited Eli. Oddly enough, Colton seemed mostly excited himself, more turned on than terrorized.

"Then I saw his dick. The motherfucker was two feet long, I kid you not. He had this crazy face, and he licked my ass and balls like a dog does, you know? Then he made me suck that big cock and it was gnarly, dude. I can't believe I choked that donkey dick down so far. But holy God, then he bent me over and fucked me like a bitch. I can't see how in the fuck he got his cock in me. Oh shit, am I bleeding? Colton asked, reaching down to his abused hole.

"No, man. It's just well-bred. You aren't tore up or anything. Damn, brother, you must be quite the bitch to attract Bigfoot to your man puss. Your stank must be the shit."

Colton laughed loudly. "Man, that is the last time I skip a shower and let my balls get that sour and smelly. Fuck me."

Eli stroked the man's hair and felt his dick swell again. Eli leaned down and kissed Colton on the side of his face and hugged him. "Glad you are okay, brother. You had me scared."

"Thanks, buddy. What a sweet guy. Yeah, just well-bred, like you said. Kind of like when I got double-dicked by Ben and Rick that time. You think anyone is gonna believe me?"

Eli shrugged. "Not sure. They might just think you got gang raped by an inmate crew or something and you were embarrassed."

"You're probably right. Shit, I would be cool with a bunch of inmates trying to fuck me, because I would be raping their ass like they never felt before. No fucking inmate is gonna cornhole me unless I say so."

Eli laughed and figured this was probably very true. "Let me help you get your pants and boots on, buddy, before everyone just thinks we've been screwing the whole night."

"Wouldn't be the first time."

Colton and Eli worked the rest of the shift close by one another, watching the dawn pink and inviting along the mountain ridges. In the distance, they could see other members of the crew hard at work. Eli let his mind wander back home again.

+ + + + + + +

As the earth had continued its circle around the sun for two more travels, Eli and his brothers began to learn to control their impulses and turned into men. Little was said of the terrible night with Makuk, and Eli devoted himself to listening and learning all that his grandfather could share, along with Sami and Reyn. They ran wild after shifting along with Sunnukkuhkau, but learned to transform back to their human form with great effort and concentration, before the moon waned. They also began to learn to shift at other times of the month. At these times, the blood fever was not burning in them and they were more lucid and in command of their faculties. The three friends would sneak away from the village in the evening and find a secluded spot in the forest. They would strip naked and watch one another shift, admiring the muscles, strength, and ferocity of their form. They would run, hunt, and play in the streams and springs. Eli loved when Sami or Reyn would nuzzle close to his large cock, balls, or ass. The boys would lick and stroke one another until they were on the verge of orgasm. Then, one of them would inevitably mount the other, sliding deep within the bowels of another Wendigo boy, riding their ass and depositing rivers of seed that would spill out and slide down their furry legs. Eli reveled in the sensations, being filled of riding a bother's ass until he exploded within. Sami and Reyn were older than Eli, tall and muscular. They were handsome and charming, with bold personalities and great senses of humor. Eli was smaller, stocky and solid. He was more serious and insightful. And what he was most proud of was that his dick bested his friends by more than an inch, both in shifted and in his human form. Many days after school, the three friends would roam in the woods to fish or gather, but many times, they ended up naked and gasping, as they sucked and fucked together in their human and shifted forms.

Eli lay between his Wendigo brothers one afternoon, spent and content from a long hour of making love together. He loved their warm bodies entwined with his. Their hands would rub and stroke one another, tickling sensitive nipples or wrapped around softening dicks, until they would swell again for another round of fucking. On this day, Reyn's face was so close to Eli's, he could feel the warm breath on his face. The boy's dark, full lips were so close to his. He reached up and touched his friend's face and lightly kissed him. Reyn's eyes flew open in surprise, but then the boy gripped his face and kissed him back, his mouth open and his tongue sliding inside Eli's. They kissed for a few moments, then Eli felt his face being pulled to the other direction, and Sami looked at him with a smirk and kissed him long and hard with a sloppy, clumsy kiss. The boys kissed and fondled one another until their cocks grew hard and Eli pushed Sami's legs apart and swallowed the fat, hard cock all the way to the thick patch of black hair, feeling Reyn do the same to his penis. Sami pulled around until Reyn's cock slid into his mouth, and the three sucked and licked until they filled one another with another thick gift of nut.

But even as his love for his new brothers deepened, Eli mourned that his relationship with Makuk had all but disappeared. He had tried many times to mend the fences with his friend, but the boy was fearful and simply would not give Eli the chance to make things right. He had listened to Sunnukkuhkau's counsel on the matter, but took small comfort from it.

"All you can do is extend the hand of fellowship and brotherly love, Eli. It will be up to Makuk to grasp it. He cannot know about your gift, yours or your other Wendigo brothers. He would not understand. His fear would grip his heart."

Then one clear autumn day, a miracle happened. As Eli was leaving school after football practice, tired and sore after a hard practice, he heard soft footsteps behind him and a hand touched his shoulder. Eli turned around, and there was Makuk. The boy had turned into a man now as well. He was tall and thin, his black hair was cut short and stuck up over his head. He now boasted a light mustache and wisps of hair on his chin. His caramel-colored eyes were still large and dark in his face. A shy grin crossed his lips.

"Hi, Eli."

Eli dropped his books and grabbed the boy in a crushing hug, pulling him close and burying his face in his hair, drinking in his scent. Eli felt his cock swell as the long-forgotten smell of his friend filled him with happiness and longing. He dismissed the foreboding and just rejoiced that his long-time friend was reaching out again.

"Oh fuck, Makuk. I have missed your mouth on my dick. Yeah, that's it buddy. Suck it. Take all of it."

Makuk repositioned himself so that his leaking penis was hovering above Eli's mouth. Eli gripped the thick seven inches and swallowed it all until Makuk was balls deep in his throat. Eli's practice with Sami and Reyn's massive pricks made deep-throating Makuk enjoyable, and he slid a wet finger into his friend's tight furry hole and probed him gently.

"Mmmmff," Makuk sighed as his ass tightened around Eli's finger.

Eli was very close to cumming when Makuk pulled away and looked at him with a wild, impassioned face. "I want to fuck you. Now!" he commanded.

Eli obeyed and assumed the position, leaned over the bed, his ass open and submitted to his friend. Makuk's mouth fastened on his ass and began to suck and probe. He pushed his tongue inside Eli's manhole, fucking him with his tongue until Eli's ass dripped with spit. Makuk leaned back and spat a wad of saliva on the tip of his rigid penis, and rested it against Eli's anus. He pushed forward hard and rammed his shaft into Eli's rectum in one hard push. Eli cried out in surprise, though the stretching and pain was nothing, compared to being penetrated by one of his Wendigo brothers.

"Fuck, brother. Take it easy. Umpf," Eli grunted.

Makuk said nothing but plowed his cock deeper and deeper into Eli's ass. His balls slapped noisily against Eli's ass as his friend fucked him hard and long. Makuk was merciless in his thrusts, no doubt still dealing with long-held anger and hurt from Eli's brutal attack. Eli grunted and swore, but secretly, his ass was happy and thrilled with the rough treatment. His Wendigo brothers bred him twice as hard, with massive cocks that felt like a fist being shoved up your ass. But he played the part, begging Makuk to stop, but reaching behind to pull him deeper and deeper into his boy cunt.

"I'm gonna cum!" Makuk shouted, unloading his balls deep within Eli's spent ass. Thick white drips of sperm leaked from the edges of Eli's anus and fell in white splats on the bedroom rug. Makuk collapsed on top of Eli, his chest wet with sweat, his belly heaving in gasps. Eli felt Makuk's penis slip out of his tired ass and flop against his crack. Eli reached around and pulled his friend into a tight embrace, kissing him deep and long. Their tongues played with one another as they kissed and groped one another.

"Fuck me, bro. Guess I had that coming," Eli said, with a smile.

"That and more. But I figure you will find out a way to make it right with a few more fucks like that." Makuk's hand gripped Eli's sack and squeezed hard.

"Shit!"

"You don't get to cum today. You are just here to service me. Suck me. I still have more nut for you," Makuk commanded.

Eli choked back his pride and ego, and opened his mouth to swallow Makuk's soft penis. He sucked it eagerly, and within a minute, it was hard again. He slid a finger into his friend's ass again and the boy rode his finger, and pumped in and out of Eli's mouth until he groaned and released his semen again. Eli swallowed the sour liquid and licked his friend's cock clean. Eli moved up and kissed Makuk again. His friend's tongue tasting the semen on his lips, and on his breath.

"My personal cocksucker," Makuk said, giving Eli's face a patronizing pat. Something about all this didn't feel right to Eli, but he chalked it up to that terrible day some years ago. He longed to be friends again, and was more than glad to humble himself and service his friend, if that made the healing come sooner.

Makuk pulled Eli onto his bed, and the two boys lay in one another's arms, softly touching and kissing. "So what's the deal with you and that Sami and Reyn from Long Haul? Are you butt buddies with them?"

"Ah, you know how it is. Bunch of horny guys with no girls around have a pretty hard time not getting busy."

"Have you even tried fucking a girl?"

Eli's face reddened. "Uh, no. Have you?"

"Sure. I've fucked three. Made the bitches suck my dick and fucked them good."

Eli wondered who in the hell was he actually talking to. He and Makuk had talked about girls and pussy many times, but it was never like some stupid misogynist rap artist. "Good for you, I guess. Are you like going out with any of them?"

"Fuck, no. Hoes like that are just a wet slit for my cock. I'm not going to be tied down. So, tell me more about these butt buddies of yours. I have seen you being all faggy with them all over town. Word is you boys suck dick 24/7, like a bitch."

Eli felt his face flush and his instincts flared hot. Something about this was really wrong. "Um, not sure who you are getting your information from, but that's a load of horseshit. Yeah, we fuck around once in a while, just like you and I did. But we are nobody's bitch."

"I even heard that you jizz-eaters are acting like you are all native and shit. I hear you let dogs and rams fuck you in the ass, run around like little girls and pretend to be a unicorn or something. Lots of guys think you need to have your ass kicked. You all need to be taught a lesson. You make people fear Indians or make white men want to hurt us."

Eli's temper flared, and his face momentarily shifted into his spirit form. It was only a split second, but he saw the fear spread across Makuk's face.

"Careful, brother. Assholes are much braver than you have regretted taunting me and my family." Eli's grin was a toothy mask of warning as he spoke.

"I don't believe you. You and your friends are just plain ole dress-wearing faggots who love to take it in the ass. Love for a real man to make you drink his piss."

In a blinding flash, Eli's arm transformed into its full Wendigo form and smashed Makuk in the chest, knocking him hard into the wall. The boy crumpled to a heap on the floor. Eli got up to leave. As he stepped into his shorts, he turned and urinated on Makuk's face and dick. He grabbed a screwdriver off the boy's desk and slid the handle roughly into Makuk's anus before leaving the room.

"I am done with you brother," he snarled.

Chapter 12

The crew made its way back to camp just before 0600. They stood in line for breakfast with black faces and hands that would not come clean with a cursory washing. The food was good and hot, about 5000 calories that they sorely needed. Eli sat quietly beside Colton and Brandon. He could barely keep his eyes open. He just wanted a bath and a bed. A thick, solid man came to join them. He had black hair literally everywhere, with sparkling blue eyes and a shiny silver band on his left hand. He leaned down and kissed Colton on the lips. A few guys from other crews stared and Eli saw one glare at the men.

"How was your night, husband?" the man said squeezing in between Colton and Eli.

"Crazy. I'll tell you later. Hey, husband, this is Eli. Chief, this the old ball and chain, Ben."

Ben smiled and wiped his hands on his napkin and shook Eli's. "Did this guy try and act like a jackass last night? You get him around new meat and he can be a real prick sometimes."

"Nah, he behaved pretty well. I think he was the one getting fucked around last night."

"Oh, really? Well, I can't wait to hear about that," Ben said between forkfuls of scrambled eggs.

Eli followed Ben, Colton, and several of the crew he hadn't met yet back to the classroom, and rummaged in his duffle bag for some fresh underwear and his flip-flops. Most of the men had stripped off their fire clothes and were moving around in sweaty underwear, a decent mixture of boxers, boxer briefs, and good ole briefs. In fact, around this group, it seemed that briefs were clearly the underwear of choice, with good ole white ones being the favorite. Most of the shorts were almost transparent now, soaked through with sweat. Pink, brown, and black backsides showed through the thin fabric as the men bent over, looking for new clothes. Men found their clean underwear or just slid the old ones off and pulled on a pair of shorts with no shirt, and headed to the showers. Eli's nose was full of the pungent scents of body odor, sweat, grime, old piss, and ass. It was like Thanksgiving. He followed Brandon's lead and pulled off everything and slid on some thin knit shorts. He noticed Bayard on the other side of the blow-up bed, bending over with his wide hairy crack showing, fat low-hanging balls far below. Bayard suddenly froze and looked between his legs, right into Eli's eyes. They flashed almost red in the dim light, locking with Eli's. The man slowly stood and turned around with a knowing look on his face. His penis was hard and the fur on his shoulders stood up in a thin line. His nostrils flared and a low rumble purred from his throat. Brandon looked around.

"What the fuck is that? I keep hearing that."

"Hearing what," Eli said, grabbing his towel.

"It's like an old Tarzan movie or something with a lion in the jungle."

"That's weird," Eli added, taking off to the bathroom, turning around to find Bayard staring straight at him, his cock now flat up against his big belly. From across the room, Eli could smell his essence radiating from his crotch. Eli swallowed hard and bolted from the room. He followed two crewmates he had not yet met (Eric and Chad, maybe). As he neared the locker room, the Latino-looking one turned around.

"You checking out my ass, rookie?" he said with a scowl.

"What? Oh, God. No." Eli sputtered.

"Well, why the fuck not? It's amazing," the man said, pushing his shorts down off his brown ass. The other man with the icy, blue eyes leaned down and took a long sniff, waving his hand in front his nose.

"That is some fucking strong funk, Señor Chad," he said. He stood up and Chad pulled up his shorts, just as a burly man from another crew came out of the locker room, freshly showered. As he passed, Eric reached over and rubbed Chad's ass lovingly, pushing his fingers up into his crack. Chad pushed his hand away.

"Stop, asshole. You're getting my stink all over these clean shorts," Chad said.

"Oh, that's the idea." Eric said back in a low voice. He looked back at Eli and extended a hand. "You must be Eli. I'm Eric. This big burrito is Chad."

The Latino man turned around and flashed a killer smile. He was the kind of man that made Eli forget pretty much everything else. He held out his hand. "Welcome, buddy."

"Thanks, guys. It's been a pleasure so far."

"You ain't seen nothing yet," Chad said, pulling Eli toward him and wrapping a big arm around his neck. He looked over at Eric. "I love little guys like this. They are so cuddly or something."

"Oh, brother." Eric said. "Better watch your cornhole, rookie. Chad hasn't poked anyone in a few days and his balls are aching."

"Like yours aren't," Chad said, pulling Eli's head to him and planting a big wet kiss on the side of his face, right as two other crew members came around the locker room corridor. They turned and stared at the men, muttering in Spanish.

"Esos tipos parecen maricones. Apuesto a que chupar la polla."

Chad turned back and shouted at them. "Usted puede lamer mis bolas gilipollas."

The men turned around and took off at a fast walk. Eli figured they weren't that used to gringo-looking guys understanding what they were saying.

"What did you say to them?" Eric asked with a laugh.

"Nothing. Just told them they could lick my balls, assholes." Eric roared, pulling off his shorts. His dick was thick and heavy, domed head and fat balls rolling in a tight sack. Chad's cock stretched down halfway to his knees, almost, was big and perfectly proportioned with a thick shaft and a wide head that was dark pink. His balls hung low and heavy and were shaved smooth, though a thick brown patch sat on top of his junk. His belly was furry along with his ass, especially the crack. Eli choked back his desire to slide his long tongue deep into that fur.

Eli dumped his towel and shorts on a bench and took his shower gear into the steamy tiled room. It was a big shower room with ten poles, four heads on each. There were six or seven men at the close poles, chatting away in Spanish. Two of them actually had on their underwear as they showered, but Eli got the impression they might be washing their clothes as well. The others washed quickly, brown uncut dicks lay on their brown balls like small snails. Eli followed Chad's big butt across the room to the poles on the far side, and turned on the water.

"Damn, rookie. Nobody's gonna give you shit with that big boy of yours between your legs," Chad said. Eli looked down. His cock was more than half hard and it was at least eight inches long.

"Ah, man. It's about like yours. That's a big burrito."

"Pay no attention to him," Eric said, running a bar of soap across his smooth belly. "He just wants to smoke your peace pipe."

Eli rolled his eyes. And still, the corny racist jokes kept coming, even if they weren't meant in a hateful way. He washed his pits and was bending down working on his legs and feet when he saw a pair of hairy legs move close, and take the shower next to him. He looked up and locked eyes once again with Bayard. The man's scent was almost more than Eli could stand without shifting. The burly, hairy man turned his back to Eli and bent over to wash his own feet. His ass was inches from Eli's face. Eli looked around and saw the others in the shower room weren't paying any attention, and he moved his nose closer into the fur-covered trench of Bayard's crack, and licked the tang and pungent odor. Bayard reached behind him and pulled one of his ass cheeks apart, and Eli daringly pushed his nose and mouth in further to the man's ass, lapping up his scent. Without words said, Bayard moved around in the dark steam, and pressed his nose and tongue deep into Eli's anus, gripping his sack and running his tongue all the way down. It was quick, just a blur, but Eli's radar was off the chart. The man stood up, and pressed his mouth against Eli's. He could taste himself on Bayard's lips and tongue. Eli looked around. No one seemed to be paying them the slightest bit of attention.

"Don't worry," Bayard said. "It's one of my things. I sort of make people not notice, deflects their attention away. They see us here, but it doesn't really register. Know what I mean?"

"That's so cool," Eli said, moving closer and licking the side of Bayard's face and beard while he dig his fingers into the man's ass. "Holy hell, brother. What are you?" Bayard's mouth found his again, and the men kissed deeply, tasting one another as their tongues moved in one another's mouths. Bayard abruptly pulled away, and began to soap up his furry belly and his now rigid penis. He grinned and leaned close to talk to Eli.

"I can only keep that up a short time. If we had kept going, all the amigos over there would have freaked out. Or come over to butt fuck us or something."

"Oh, wow. Well, I would really like to talk to you later," Eli said, running the soap into his balls and erect penis, trying to make it mash down.

"Rookie, that is a lost cause. You might as well just rub one out right here," Chad said, his own penis hard and beautiful. Eli watched Eric bend down to scrub his feet, and actually let the tip of Chad's dick run across his lips. *Fuck that's hot,* Eli thought.

"Yeah, I know. I better take care of it soon," Eli said with a grin.

"Buddy, I have a feeling Bayard's gonna take care of you with a big ole 69, finished off with a fudge pack. Hey, what happened to Colton last night? I heard him yammering on about getting butt raped by Bigfoot."

"That's funny. I think I look a lot more like a hobbit," Eli said with a big smile. The men laughed.

"Look who's a smart ass. Doesn't surprise me. Colton's a big baby when he's riding a pole. God knows he whimpers like a bitch when he's riding mine," Chad said, sliding a soapy hand back and forth on his solid erection. "What do you say, rookie. Want to take a ride?"

"Can we at least get back to the sleeping room?" Eli said.

"I think you're gonna be plenty busy in there. I'll get up in that sweet ass soon enough, brother." Chad said, reaching over, sending two soapy fingers deep into Eli's ass. A low rumble chortled from Bayard's throat.

"Sorry, man. Indigestion," he said.

The crewmates finished up, high-fiving several others that were just coming in. Eli got introduced to an older firefighter named Tom, with a long pony tail and bushy beard that curiously was sporting a thick, silver cock ring. He was with two younger firefighters, Ian and Aaron, who seemed about Eli's age. These boys smell like they need to nut bad, Eli thought sniffing their sweaty bodies. The young guys had semi-hard cocks that looked ready to pop with just a bit of attention. Eli drew in one last long breath before wrapping his towel around himself and flip-flopping back to the crew day sleep area.

When he opened the door, the cool air-conditioned air was sweet. The facilities unit had done a good job blocking off the daylight from the big windows. Eli could just make out the scattered sleepers around the room. As his eyes adjusted, his senses picked on a new sound and smell in the far corner. He peered in that direction and saw the sturdy back and ass of a firefighter he thought was named Rick, pumping in and out of the butt of a husky, veteran firefighter who was very softly moaning into a pillow. He turned in another direction, and saw Eric and Chad drop their towels and lay back head to toe on the air mattress they shared. Their heads began to bob up and down as they slurped and sucked on one another in a deep 69.

A large arm draped around Eli's chest and down to his cock, gripping it in a soft tug. Eli looked around and saw Jake, the crew boss, smiling. The man's face rested against Eli's, and he breathed slowly as he stroked the rookie's erection.

"Looks like you are pretty comfortable with all this," Jake whispered. "You and Jesse fuck on the way back yesterday?"

"Yeah. It was really fun."

"That's good. I had a feeling you were going to be a great addition. Sounds like Big isn't going to be rejoining us, so if you are able, we might just pick you up full time for the rest of the season, if you're interested."

Eli leaned against the large man and spread his legs a bit wider, feeling the man's fingers slide past his sack and tease his manhole. He turned his face and felt Jake's warm lips connect with his as his fingers slid inside him.

"I'd like that, Jake. Feels like I'm home here."

"By the way, Bayard had a quick chat with me. Seems like the two of you need to get lost for a short time tomorrow night. That will work just as long as you stick together and follow his lead. I'll let him fill in the details." The man moved in closer behind Eli, his penis rubbing up and down the young man's crack. "We are really lucky to have this sleeping situation. Doesn't often work out like this, one of the reasons I was willing to do the night shift. Guess you can tell we fuck one another a lot. We just keep it quiet and respectful in here. When we are back home or in your own time, you can get crazy. We keep it pretty vanilla in here. With you being new and all, I bet a bunch of the guys are going to want to dip their cock into your honey pot. If you aren't into it for any reason, you just have let them know. No one is gonna force fuck you…unless you are wanting to be forced." Jake said with a chuckle. He spat a small gob into his hand, and Eli felt the man slide it into his ass. The head of Jake's penis slid in afterwards, thick and solid.

"I'm really tired, but I need to bust a nut right before I sleep, and your ass is irresistible." Jake slowly penetrated Eli from behind. Eli lifted his leg and rested it on a window ledge as Jake fucked fast and hard, gripping his waist. Eli looked to his side and saw that Colton and Ben were staring, Colton balls deep in his husband. Ben flashed a thumbs-up Eli's way as Jake continued to pound his pussy. Soft smacks filled the air from Eli and Jake. They were echoed back from Ben and Colton and Rick and whoever he was plowing. The room reeked of ass juice and clean sweat. Jake gripped Eli hard and drove inside him one last time, grunting a release deep inside. Jake kissed the short man one last time, and patted him on the butt.

"Thanks, buddy. Get some sleep," Jake said.

Eli turned back to his bed to see Bayard already there, naked and stroking his thick penis, the heavy foreskin sliding all the way over the large tip and then back down. His hairy chest and belly were like a smooth carpet. Eli slid into the bed beside him and let the man wrap him into his warm embrace.

"Hi again, buddy." Bayard smiled and his finger slid into Eli's asshole. He brought it out, slid into his mouth. "Yep, tastes like the boss for sure," he whispered. "Figured he would tap your ass. Just like a fucking alpha."

"What was he talking about, you and me needing some time to get lost tonight?"

Bayard's face moved close. He softly kissed Eli, and then licked the side of his face with a long wet tongue. Eli's cock swelled hard against the furry belly as the man continued to lick him like a mother with her young. His smell was intoxicating to Eli, who joined with him in the licking and nuzzling. Eli had never experienced such scent. It was powerful, magical, and primal, like the connection he had with Sami and Reyn, but this was different, he thought. In the dim light, Bayard seemed to shimmer somewhere between the here and the there.

"Okay. I can tell you are like me in some kind of way. Care to tell me more, bro?" Eli said.

"Can't say too much in here. Too many Nosy Parkers. You ever hear of a Kelpie?"

Eli shook his head. "Can't say I have. Dare I guess you are some kind of shifter?"

Bayard smiled. "Just like you, kiddo. I could smell you a mile away. You are a fucking powerful one at that. Werewolf?" Bayard whispered into Eli's ear.

"Wendigo."

"Motherfucker," Bayard whispered back in awe. "You have to shift tomorrow night, right?"

"Yeah. You?"

"It's controllable for me, but it hurts like hell if I don't. So yeah, I'm fucking shifting too."

"And Jake knows?"

"Had to tell him a few years ago, just no other way. It freaked him out pretty big when I revealed it. I took him with me out in the woods one day and shifted in front of him. He almost shit himself. But he was also fucking turned on like crazy. He doesn't get fucked very often, but I bred his ass while I was shifted, he moaned like a little bitch. We've fucked a dozen times since then, mostly me topping him for sure when I was shifted."

"Goddamn," Eli whispered. The men turned toward the sound of the couple next to them. Brandon was gripping Jesse's shoulders as he slid himself up and down on the blond man's erection. The men kissed deeply as Jesse plowed his boyfriend deeply inside his stretched ass.

"Those two are in love, but Jesse likes fucking so much, I think they fight a lot. He tapped your sweet hole, didn't he?"

"No – I fucked the shit out of him though."

"Dude! That is awesome. I think it's cool when smaller guys top big ones like him. He's a sweet guy. I've enjoyed breeding him a couple of times and fuck, he can ream you good when he's fucking you."

"I can tell. So maybe I should know, but I don't. What the fuck is a Kelpie?"

"Scottish shifter. Kind of lame sometimes. Mostly I manifest as a horse with a really long mane and a fucking huge dick. I can also become a half horse – half fish and breathe underwater."

"Shit. That's pretty great. You start shifting when…"

"My balls dropped. Yep. The minute the testosterone started flowing and my cum started squirting, so did my shifting. Same with you?"

"Exactly."

"So, a Wendigo. You grow horns and claws and a wolf head and all that?"

"Yep. And a fucking huge horse cock too," Eli said with a laugh. Next door, Brandon cried out that he was cumming.

"Kind of hard to sleep in here until everyone gets their nut off. But with this bunch, that doesn't take too long," Bayard added.

All around the room, the soft sounds of snoring were slowly overtaking the muted grunts of fucking and bodies smacking together. The perfume of the room was thick with semen and clean sweat, and it made Eli's cock drool in desire.

"I want to see you shift tomorrow. I want to run with you," Bayard whispered. His cock rubbed against Eli's penis in soft, long strokes. The men ground their crotches together, fingers sliding in and out of warm assholes.

"I am really relieved. I didn't know what I was going to do. I want to run with you too, brother."

"I want us to breed tomorrow. Can I mate with you while we're shifted?"

"Yeah. I'm kind of crazy, though. You okay with it getting kind of rough?"

"It better be rough, dude. You're a fucking monster after all. Hey, we need to sleep. Let's wait until tomorrow to fuck, buddy. But my balls are about to bust. Suck me off? I'll swap you."

"Thought you'd never ask." Eli slid down and took Bayard's penis in his hand and played with the loose foreskin, slipping easily back and forth over his beer-can-sized cock. It smelled clean and male in every way. He swallowed his erection all the way to his thick brown pubes and let his throat get used to the thick member. Eli began to suck and work on the knob of Bayard's penis with his tongue. It took less than two minutes and the muscled, burly man was gripping his head and unloading a thick, sour, strange, and delicious blast of semen into Eli's mouth. Eli swallowed every drop and milked Bayard's penis for the last drops as the man softly moaned. He leaned forward and took Eli's cock into his mouth and sucked long and slow, massaging the boy's testicles and moving down to slurp Eli's smooth asshole before moving back to the cock that was growing thicker and longer by the minute. But as Eli's dick swelled and grew well past twelve inches, Bayard's face seemed to stretch and the man easily swallowed every inch of Eli's penis, as he slid his wet fingers in and out of the boy's hole. Eli gripped Bayard's head and silently orgasmed into his lapping mouth, with blast after blast of sperm.

Bayard moved up and kissed Eli deeply, letting the load in his mouth flow back and forth between them. "You taste like magic, brother. Magic and fucking nitro or something. I can't wait to breed with you tonight."

The men fell into a deep sleep, along with the rest of the crew, soft snores and the occasional grunt of a penetrated ass filling the quiet, cool room.

Chapter 13

Eli dreamed and his mind flew back home once again. It was late October and the nights were growing cold. More than once, Eli had woken to frost on the ground and the smell of snow in the air. After school and football practice, he had taken to spending all his time again with Sami and Reyn. Makuk's words haunted him and he found himself more intent than usual with being the top player in their games sexual escapades together. He was more vicious and menacing, snarling, slashing, and fucking with such ferocity. Eli's grandfather actually slapped him in the face after Eli spoke disrespectfully to him after an argument. The slap caused Eli to shift and slash out at Sunnukkuhkau. The older man had shifted and grabbed Eli and slammed him through the wall of the house in a sudden, deafening roar.

"If you are only going to be ruled by your passions and your dick, then you will not live long, my son. You must rise above this petty hatred. Makuk simply wounded you back as you once wounded him. He can yet be your friend, of that I am sure."

Eli listened but deep down, he honestly felt his grandfather's wisdom was not correct this time. Something about Makuk had felt off. The sweet openness of his friend had been replaced with a cold deception that concealed little of his loathing and inherent anger. Eli had grown up listening to other boys talk about seeing spirit creatures and a Wendigo was certainly one of the most celebrated, feared, and boasted about. More than one of his acquaintances had claimed to see a shifted Wendigo. One boy in particular, Leo Black, swore that a Wendigo had abducted his brother and raped him, and later tore the boy's head from his shoulders. The story sounded fantastic like a rumor gone mad. But from what he really knew, could the boy be telling the truth? He had been stopped from killing himself several times already. What would he do if one time, Sunnukkuhkau was not there to save him?

Eli's grandfather had planned a winter hunt for the following weekend. The moon would be full and since it was right before the white man's Thanksgiving, it was a time for the native men to celebrate the season in their own way - hunting and feasting. Sunnukkuhkau had promised the boys to talk about women and how they might find a wife who could understand what it meant to be mated to a Wendigo. The boys could talk of little else. Their own understanding and experience with women and the mysteries of the pussy were topics of long discussion. Sami was convinced that to a Wendigo, a woman's pussy would be filled with monstrous shark like teeth that would chomp off a boy's cock as he thrust it deep within the girl. Reyn roared and told Sami he was utterly full of shit, but Eli wondered if Sami might be onto something. Not that he believed the idea of a vagina with teeth, but might the magic of that woman be awakened and attack the Wendigo in some way to fend off an unwanted breeding? It was hard to know for sure.

Eli knew his grandfather was respected in the tribe and small town of Christmas, Michigan. But sometimes, he watched the eyes of the men or women and saw something else besides respect. Fear, maybe. Sami, Reyn, and Eli had faced typical mean kids at school, kids that would challenge them or mock them for no reason. It took a lot of control and restraint not to attack or make them pay. But Eli's grandfather was a patient and thorough teacher, and little by little, the boys were becoming thoughtful men who reveled in their bodies and gifts and knew how to keep that quiet and separate from the rest of their lives.

The weekend came, and Eli and his good friends loaded up in Sunnukkuhkau's old Suburban along with one of his grandfather's closest friends, Joel. They talked and joked as they wound their way deep into the forest for their weekend. Eli lost track of how many twists and turns they took. But more than once, Eli looked back because he swore they were being followed, even out here in the middle of nowhere.

After almost two hours of driving, Sunnukkuhkau pulled off the logging road into a thick canopy of trees. The frozen ground made the driving good, with only a small dusting of snow here and there so far. The air was icy as they scrambled out and made camp. The big elk hunting tent went up fast and, with Eli's grandfather's skill, was warm with a wood stove cranking away before they knew it. The boys had made fun of the man bringing the heavy stove along, but now were praising the man for his foresight. The boys continued to set up the rest of camp according to Eli's grandfather's instructions, and soon, the sleeping mats, food, and other supplies were sorted out.

"The celebration has now begun boys. Remove your clothes. You will not need them again until we return to the village. This weekend, we shift and run. We howl, hunt, and tear. And we rut, and mate, and breed. My brother and I will run with you, now that you are men. We will share our wisdom and knowledge. After this weekend, you will begin to find your way in this world as men and Wendigo."

Eli and his friends stripped off their clothes and stood arm in arm in front of the older men. Joel was shorter and thicker than Sunnukkuhkau, but his cock lay as large and heavy as the bigger man. The older men began to chant. The boys joined in. Soon, they moved in a circle around the tent, celebrating their spirit and gift. The chant rose in volume and temp until the men and boys were shouting and running. Sweat gleamed on their chests. Eli's balls felt like they were going to snap off as they bounced around. The men burst from the tent out into the frigid air, but the frost felt like nothing to Eli's feet. He wanted to rut and breed. He could taste blood already. Then altogether, they cried out and the men, young and old, shifted. One by one, they transformed. Antlers sprouted, muzzles grew and snarled, cocks swelled, and fur and claws sprang forth.

As the pack turned to run into the night, the stillness was shattered by a blast that echoed through the forest. Joel fell to the ground in a heap, half his head missing. Sunnukkuhkau shrieked and turned, but a second blast rocketed into the pack, and Reyn fell at Sami's feet, his chest blown apart.

The rest of the men bolted in three different directions as shots rang out. Eli's blood fever boiled over into a rage he had never felt before. He tore through the forest more silently than ever, a whisper, as he flew through the frozen night. He smelled the killers, and his senses locked in to them like a laser. As he flanked them, he could hear his grandfather and Sami moving like falling leaves in the still air. As Eli moved near, he crouched low and slithered forward. The man was there, weapon in hand. Blind like a coward, Eli poised to strike. Then from the side, the blur of a shadow moved past with a deafening snarl. The weapon discharged and dropped to the ground, along with the killer's head. A fountain of blood bubbled up from the stump of his neck and sprayed the white ground as the body fell forward.

Eli's nose filled with the scent of blood and death. He wanted to kill worse than ever before. But danger was still all around. He stayed low and moved forward. He lifted his head and sniffed. The killers were still around. He moved close to the scent, staying low and concealed in the undergrowth. From his left, Eli sensed more movement. He saw another hunter move into the silver light, and watched the shape of Sami race from the shadow with a deafening snarl. Eli barked a warning, but it was too late. As Sami reared up to pounce and kill, a third hunter emerged from the darkness, and fired. The blast cut Sami almost in half, dropping the boy like a quail in mid-flight.

Eli shrieked, and tore from the shadows toward the first hunter, claws extended. Eli caught the man by the neck and ripped the windpipe from his throat in one blur. A hot gasp filled the air. With a twist, Eli snapped the man's neck like a dove's. He dropped to the ground. Eli's senses were clouded with the blood and the fury. Too late, he heard the third man step back into the light from hiding. His eyes opened wide as he saw the contorted face of Makuk. The boy lifted the weapon to his shoulder, with a clear shot to Eli.

"I knew you were a freak, a monster that wanted to rape me again. You won't be hurting me or any other. Go back to hell!" he screamed as he fired.

A roar echoed along with the weapon, and a massive shape flew in front of Eli before dropping to the ground with a thud. Eli's world imploded. With a ferocity beyond any he had ever felt, he flew forward and grabbed Makuk in his claws. The boy screamed and beat at his hands in utter futility. With a single swipe, Eli slashed Makuk's clothing to shreds, and it fell to the ground like ashes from a fire. He gripped the young man's legs and pushed them open wide. In one brutal shove, he penetrated his old friend with a massive cock that ripped his ass apart. He slashed at Makuk's groin and held his severed genitals in his razor-like talons, before shoving the organs into the man's open mouth. Then with a mighty growl, Eli came like a geyser into Makuk's ruined anus before dropping the boy to the ground. Eli ran to the fallen form nearby. Eli transformed into his human form, and knelt and cradled Sunnukkuhkau in his arms. The clear, brown eyes opened, a gush of blood coming from his mouth.

"*Nimishomis!* Please Papa. Don't leave me," Eli sobbed. His tears dropped onto the pale face he held and mixed with the blood. "I'm sorry, Papa. I should have been faster."

"Eluwilussit. All that matters is that you are safe. Remember, you are Holy One. The Great Spirit has so much for you. I will miss watching you become the man you are destined to be. Don't let hate push out love. Follow your heart and dreams. You are made for greatness."

Eli sobbed harder. "I can't make it without you, Papa."

"You can. You are full of knowledge and power. Follow the old ways… in new ways, my son. I have loved you so." The man held his hand to Eli's head and began a blessing chant, while Eli's tears streamed down. "Teach this to your own son, Eli. Just as you teach him to be Wendigo." Eli watched his grandfather's eyes close and open with a start, staring deep into Eli's face. "I should have listened to you about Makuk. Go end that fucker," he snarled, then slipped away.

Eli sobbed anew and held his grandfather to his chest while he rocked back and forth. Finally, he laid the man down and stood. He looked across the clearing to where the crumpled form of Makuk lay, gripping his groin. He walked over and stood above his old friend.

"I would have loved you forever. You chose fear instead of love, brother. Be warm in hell, niijii." Eli shifted, watching Makuk's face fill with fear. He struck like an adder, ripping Makuk's throat open, his blood gushing over Eli's snout. He drank deeply and lapped at his friend's blood until the light left his eyes.

+ + + + + + +

Eli's eyes fluttered open, adjusting to the dimness of the room, and almost screamed. Bayard's face and bushy beard were hovering just a few inches away from his nose.

"Jesus!" Eli hissed. "You scared me."

"Dude, you must have been having a hell of a dream. I thought you were going to rip my head off. I kept trying to keep you quiet. Everything okay, buddy?"

"Yeah," Eli lied. He let Bayard wrap him into his arms and tried to calm himself, listening to Bayard's breathing as a tear slid down his face.

"Will you tell me about it tonight, brother?" Bayard quietly asked. He tenderly slid his hand through Eli's hair and down the side of his face, pressing his furry belly close to Eli's smooth one. His tenderness was like an ointment.

"If you want. You might not want to snuggle up so much after that though."

Chapter 14

Evening shadows were long by the time Eli had finished telling his story to Bayard. The men were assigned mop-up patrol, instead of the direct attack or burnout duties of the rest of the crew. It left them on their own for the night, just what Jake had promised. Bayard listened intently, not reacting even when Eli confessed to killing his long-time friend. The firefighters stood on the edge of a landing, looking out toward the active burn of the fire, watching the day wind down to purple evening.

Eli felt empty and spent from sharing the story. It was the first time he had ever told it all. It was like scratching a scab, satisfying and painful at the same time. Bayard rubbed his neck and just listened. It was exactly what Eli needed. The men stood quietly for a long time before Bayard spoke.

"I can't begin to know how you feel, buddy. But I think I do know this: you didn't murder anyone. You defended yourself and tried to save your friends and family. Those fuckers got what they deserved. They just messed with the wrong magical beast."

Eli looked at Bayard, and burst out laughing. "Magical beast. Oh brother."

"What?" Bayard said. "Okay, mythical Algonquin monster... what should I say?"

"You think we are gonna get in trouble for leaving our job tonight to run?" Eli asked, picking up his Pulaski, and carefully spinning it in his hand like a baton.

"Nah, there's not much to do here. We can hit the area with the IR camera, but my eyes tell me there's not really any hotspots left. Jake left us here on purpose." Bayard stretched his arms wide and scratched his balls. "It's almost 2200. Close enough, don't you think? I want to shift and breed your ass, brother." Bayard bent down and unlaced his boots, and walked back to the pickup. A few moments later, he came around the front of the vehicle, naked and erect. He walked on the rough ground like his feet were made of leather. Eli stood there, with his clothes in a neat pile beside his boots, the wind catching his long black hair and whipping it across his face. His cock was heavy and hard, a long drip of pre-cum hung from the tip. Bayard moved close and took the short man in his arms and kissed him long, tasting his scent and essence. Eli slipped to his knees and took Bayard's thick cock into his mouth and sucked him, burying his nose in the brown furry crotch. He gripped Bayard's ass and pulled the man in and out of his mouth, relishing the taste and tang of his flesh. Eli sucked and moved between Bayard's low-slug sack, bathing his balls with his tongue, moving underneath to flick his tongue against the furry trench and his asshole. He tasted the man and felt his desire grow. Bayard pulled him upright and swallowed Eli's penis to the hilt, a guttural gagging sound in the back of his throat. Bayard was orally skilled, his mouth and tongue thrilling Eli's cock to almost the point of climax in just a few moments. The soft, furry face nuzzled his sack and probed his ass apart to penetrate his boyhole with his tongue until he was dripping and longing. Bayard ate Eli's hole deep, and let the scent fill his nose and mouth with masculinity and magic. He stood up to face Eli, their rigid poles touching one another.

Wordlessly, the men began to shimmer, vibrate, and transform. Eli's bloodlust boiled as he watched Bayard drop to all fours and grow into a sleek chestnut stallion, with a mane and tail that reached the ground. He reared up, his cock extended, slapping wet and loud against his belly. The fucker looked two feet long. Eli morphed, feeling his face grow along with his claws and hair and cock. He stood monstrous and erect before Bayard. He moved his muzzled face close, licking the stallion's muzzle and reaching underneath to grip the fat horse cock. Mentally, Eli spoke to Bayard in a connection that shifted creatures could.

The shifted pair moved back into the thick fir trees, and found a small clearing that stared up into the purple sky, peppered with stars and a haunting full moon. Eli leapt up on a fallen, old growth log and presented his ass to Bayard as he lifted his face to the sky and roared, his antlers shaking heavy and grand on his head. His fat cock stretched down along with his sack low and loose. Bayard's muzzle touched his ass and a thick, hot tongue began to lick and eat the presented hole. The tongue was like a thick snake pushing its way inside of Eli, lapping at his anus and balls until they ran like rivers. In a flash, the stallion reared and his heavy hooves rested on Eli's shoulders, his dripping horse cock rubbed hard against the muscle, and then penetrated all the way inside until Eli thought he was being sawn in half. But his ass adjusted and the cock began to pummel him like a sledgehammer. The heat and froth from Bayard fed Eli's desires, and he pushed the horse cock deeper and deeper inside him. He was being fucked apart and yet, there was no pain, no tearing. Just sex, and power, and seed. Bayard's sperm filled Eli's ass like a fire extinguisher, thick clots of horse sperm pouring from the edges of Eli's stretched rectum. This was being bred like only a shifter could be. His bloodlust boiled over as the stallion slammed inside him one last time, and Eli roared again. His cock could wait no longer.

In a flash, Eli slid the massive appendage from his anus, and he ran. The two ran like the wind through the forest, leaping and darting through the thick growth. First one, then the other, taking the lead. Eli could feel his thighs wet and slick with Bayard's seed leaking from his spent hole, and he loved it. The pair ran past rivers and mountain lakes that shimmered silver in the full moon. Forest creatures froze and scurried away, not daring to move into the wake of the beings that ran with authority in their domain. Eli's nose filled with the blood and scent of so much quarry. He would have to feed soon. As the pair exploded into a thicket, a startled young buck took flight. Eli and Bayard were on him in an instant. With one flash, the Wendigo tore away his larynx, and the beast fell almost silently to the forest floor. The creatures descended on the deer and gorged themselves on blood and meat, thanking the Great Spirit for providing the sustenance.

After feeding, Eli felt the bloodlust pounding in his ears. He began to circle the stallion, his harsh breath rattling, his claws rigid. The stallion stamped and snorted, tossing his head and mane in a fierce circle. Eli charged at the beast and climbed on its back, as it tore away in a blur. The Wendigo gripped the foamy flanks of the stallion with his muscled legs, as the steed shot through the forest at a run. The Wendigo sank gently into the flesh of the stallion, just enough to inflict the smallest pain. The pair moved into a cool draw where a mountain creek burbled over rocks and ferns. The stallion finally stopped, his sides heaving. He spread his back legs wide and let a frothy blast of piss shoot from his cock into the mossy ground. The Wendigo slid from the stallion's back and moved to its rear. He moved the long, glossy tail to the side, and let his hot tongue bathe the pulsing muscle. The stallion remained crouched and tossed his head more as Eli's tongue penetrated Bayard's anus. Eli retracted his claws on his right hand and slid three fingers into the pulsing orifice. The stallion neighed and snorted again as Eli's other hand reached down and gripped the flopping penis, stroking in quickly before slipping his entire hand into the stallion's asshole. The beast stood stock still, pushing further and further back on the Wendigo's hand. Eli positioned himself behind the stallion, balanced on a rise on the ground that pulled him level with the horse's backside. He roared and plowed all twenty inches of his engorged cock into the stallion's lubed anus. Bayard shrieked and reared, but remained in place as Eli fucked hard and fast, gripping the chestnut flanks, his massive balls pounding into the stallion's rear. Eli turned his head to the sky and roared and thrust forward, impaling himself deep into Bayard's bowels, unloading hot streams of semen, again and again, into the stallion's stretched anus. Eli fell to the forest floor in a heap, shifting into his human form.

He awoke a few moments later with his head in Bayard's lap. His crewmate looked concerned and was scooping up cool water with this palm, and tipping then into Eli's parched face and mouth.

"You okay, brother? Fuck, man. That was the most wicked sex I have ever had in my life. Feels like you just drove a Type 6 engine up my shitter. Damn. My ass is literally pouring with nut, just gushing out like a fire hose."

"You reamed me out pretty good too, bro. I know you filled up my keister with that horse spunk of yours too. Fuck, your cock was so huge."

"Yours, too. I'm not sure a stallion normally takes it in the ass like that," Bayard laughed. "Must not be a lot of gay horses. You feel like you can stand up now?"

"I think so. Shit, we must have run so far. It's going to take a while to get back. You have any idea where we are?"

"Not a clue, other than it's definitely in the opposite direction of the fire. No worries, but we'll have to shift back and run to get home in time." Bayard helped Eli up and steadied him. The naked men held on to one another for a moment, pressing faces against one another. Bayard pulled back and saw that Eli was quietly crying.

"Hey, buddy. It's okay. I got you. You aren't alone. I know you're sad and everything, but I'm here, and I'm not going anywhere."

"Yeah, but what happens when this fire is over?"

"You heard Jake, he wants to keep you on."

"But I'm like homeless back home. I was literally staying in a shelter before I got the fire job."

Bayard kissed Eli long and hard, tasting the salty tears on his tongue. "You're not homeless anymore, buddy. I love you, you idiot. Come stay with me, let me be your person, your boyfriend... whatever."

Eli sniffed and looked at the sweet, bearded man, and touched his face. "I've always wanted a horse," he said.

Bayard's eyes narrowed. "You little shit, you better watch that. I'm not your fucking My Pretty Pony. And just so you know, you're the only motherfucker whom I will ever let his whole goddamn fist up my asshole."

Eli laughed. "I can't believe we found each other. Sunnukkuhkau told me I would find my soul mate. I don't know if I ever believed him. When I'm with you, I feel like my heart is finding a way to be whole again. I love you too, brother. Whatever the fuck a Kelpie is, I love that too."

The men slid into the cold stream and bathed together before climbing out on the bank and sucking one another until they drank their fill of seed. Eli looked up at the moon and actually smiled, for the first time in so long, not hating the orb. The men moved up on the ridge and shifted again, and tore through the night beside the other, racing toward the dawn, and a new life together.

~~The End~~

Here is a sample from another story you may enjoy:

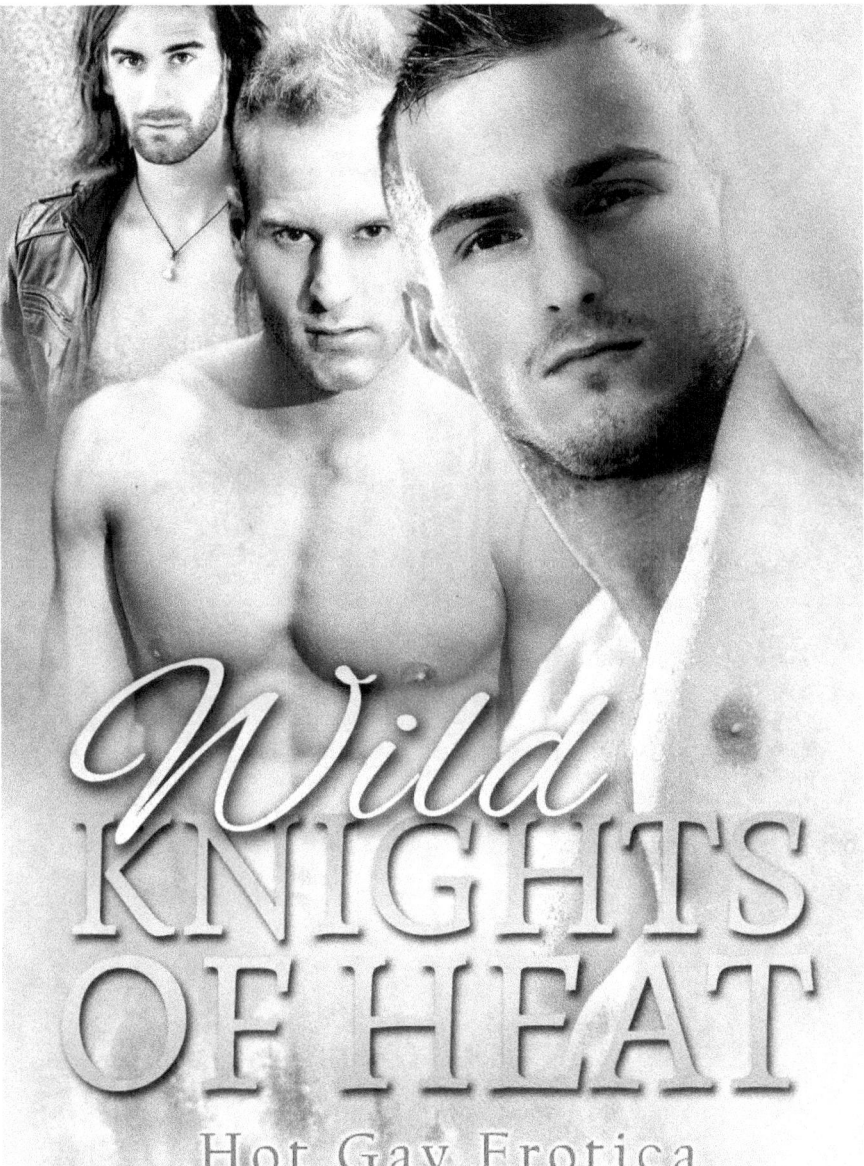

Wild
KNIGHTS
OF HEAT

Hot Gay Erotica

ANGUS MACGREGOR

"Hey, you think those boys are still awake?"

"You want more nut after all that?"

"I need to fuck a rookie tonight."

"Well, they are just down the hall. Tell them to get their asses in here."

Five minutes later, Sam's face was buried so deep in Ian's meaty ass it looked like his whole head was sliding inside. The rookie was on his belly, reaching behind to part his ass cheeks wide to let Sam have as much access as possible to his well-used hole. Sam pulled the boy's cock toward him so he could alternately suck the fat round head and Ian's smooth nutsack before drilling his hungry tongue deep into the young man's asshole yet again. The married man's face was wet with saliva as he feasted on the boy's hole, pulling it wide apart and probing the furry rosebud with his darting tongue.

While Sam dined on Ian's ass, Tom pushed Aaron's large, muscular legs apart and up toward his shoulders. The rookie's manhole was slippery with spit and Tom's fingers easily penetrated his muscle. His soft groans filled the dark room as two, three, then four fingers slid within the boy's pussy. Tom bathed his balls with his tongue, holding each one and sucking it gently at first, then harder until the rookie's belly quivered and he groaned anew. Aaron's penis leaked a steady flow of cock snot, a long string of silvery sweetness that dripped from the tiny lips of his throbbing cock, making a large sticky pool on his furry belly. Tom supped and sucked the rookie's hole and cock, feeling the tight virgin muscle give way until his four large fingers slid in and out with rapid ease. Aaron pulled around and took Tom's rigid pole into his mouth and swallowed it until his lips rested against the man's chrome ring. His eyes watered as Tom's cock stretched his mouth and filled his throat, his gag reflex coming in waves. Aaron looked over and saw Sam feeding Ian his thick penis, fucking his face with long deliberate strokes that buried his member deep into the rookie's mouth, flattening his nose into his thick nest of black pubes.

"Ok rook, breeding time," Sam hissed, pulling his cock out and slapping it noisily against Ian's soggy anus. The boy's eyes closed as the man's thick penis penetrated his hole and slid fully inside resting the man's gut and heavy sack against Ian's round ass. "Goddamn, I love plowing probie pussy," Sam said as began a rhythmic pumping into Ian's shitter.

"Oh my fucking God," Ian shouted as the pounding continued.

Tom pulled his cock out of Aaron's mouth, gripped the boy's thick, hairy ankles and let the tips of his penis rub against the spent asshole. Tom rocked back and forth twice and then pressed forward until the thick head of his cock split Aaron's sphincter. Tom's ass was a blur as he pounded again and again, deeply into Aaron's boyhole, ignoring the cries of pain. He finally leaned forward and pressed his mouth tightly against Aaron's, smothering out the shouts with deep kisses. Tom fucked the boy until he emptied his nuts again inside the ruined hole, white semen leaking from the stretched anus. Aaron's arms were tight around Tom's neck, the young man's kisses were deep and hungry. Across the bed, Sam shouted and ejaculated his thick load into Ian's spent asshole before collapsing on the sweaty rookie. Ian turned his head toward Sam and felt the man's tongue slide inside his open mouth.

"You are smokin' hot, buddy. I love fucking a rookie's ass like yours so much. Goddamn, you love getting pounded." With that, Sam slid down and began to lick and suck Ian's cum-filled hole while the rookie writhed and moaned.

"I'm gonna nutt," he gasped.

Sam flipped him over and gripped the young man's penis as it erupted blast after blast of thick semen into the married man's goateed mouth. When Aaron saw that, he felt his own orgasm explode and Tom lapped the hot sperm up from his hairy belly and leaking dick. The men lay still on the king-sized bed, soft sounds of kisses and breathing filled the warm bedroom. Aaron lay his head on Tom's big hairy chest and listened to the man's heart beat strong against his ear.

"I kind of love laying here like this," Aaron whispered, listening to Ian and Sam's soft kissing against his back. His ass was rubbing gently against his friend's. He reached over and let his hand slide down his butt to his legs and back up. Ian's hand found his and slid his fingers into Aaron's. Tom's large hand brushed against Aaron's face and kissed the rookie again, smiling at the sweaty face, tasting the mix of sperm and salt on his tongue.

"I kind of love it too, little buddy. Always have. You boys mean the world to me."

"You can fuck me any time you want, Tom," Aaron said.

Tom rested his nose against the rookie's nose. "You can count on it."

If you enjoyed this sample then look for **<u>Wild Knights of Heat</u>**.

Also by this Author:

The Hotshot Brotherhood

Brokeback Buddies

Drive My Engine, Rookie

South Patrol Pounding

Shower of Power

The Pardoned Series, Book 1 - Rise From Abyss

The Pardoned Series, Book 2 - Rescued

Wild Knights of Heat

Son Swap

Bad Sheriff

Here Comes Trouble

Fighting My Instincts

From the Author

WANT FREE COPIES OF MY BOOKS?
Just visit my blog and download free copies of my books:
http://angus-macgregor.awesomeauthors.org/angus-macgregor/

If you enjoyed any of my books then please share the love and click like on my books in Amazon. Your reviews are greatly appreciated.

One Last Thing, For Kindle Readers...

When you turn the page, Kindle will give you the opportunity to rate this book and share your thoughts on Facebook and Twitter. If you enjoyed my writings, would you please take a few seconds to let your friends know about it? Because... when they enjoy they will be grateful to you and so will I.

Thank You!

Angus MacGregor
angus_macgregor@awesomeauthors.org

About the Author

Angus MacGregor resides with his family in Oregon and Hawaii. Along with his passion for writing, Angus enjoys growing orchids, snorkeling and hiking.

Angus has worked as a school teacher, a financial analyst, and a small business developer. He currently works as a writer and supports firefighting efforts by working on wildfires in the US during the summer months. In addition to his adult erotica books, Angus has recently completed his first book of mainstream fiction.

"I love seeing what the Universe has in store for me as I create this reality. I love my life and the blessings of all the people and gifts that surround me. I wish peace and blessings to all my readers."

WANT FREE COPIES OF MY BOOKS?

Just visit my blog and download free copies of my books:
http://angus-macgregor.awesomeauthors.org/angus-macgregor/

www.ingramcontent.com/pod-product-compliance
Lightning Source LLC
Chambersburg PA
CBHW071416170626
46811CB00003B/1422